IN THIS CITY, WHERE IT RAINS

LYNDSEY CROAL

LUNA NOVELLA #25

Contents

The House

Tair House sits at the edge of the city's memory, on a cobbled street by an ancient cemetery, where dead leaves rustle, and the only birds that speak their secrets to the stillness are crows, rooks, and magpies. The grand house has stood here a long time, built with aged stone and covered in vines of dead ivy that creep up crumbling walls and break their way into even the tiniest of crevice and crack. Overgrown and dying shrubs line the grounds, while thickets of brambles grow over every pathway, seeping blood-red juices into the earth.

In the city, it always rains, but here, there is a different kind of cold that creeps into everything. Thick clouds gather above but never quite break. A permanent frost dapples windows, obscuring the inside. In this house, darkness lurks. Shadowy figures linger, just out of sight. The house holds all of it close because it remembers what it has lost, and what it could still lose.

To anyone looking, the house would appear abandoned — but it is not so. Its current owners are as elusive as the rain — the Logan family. Tair House knows all about them — knows their secrets, knows what they've done. The house does not believe it is owned so much that it owns them. Still, the house is fond of its inhabitants, the shadowy and solid figures alike.

Xavier Logan is a wealthy man with grey eyes and an ice-cold stare. He dresses in tweed trousers and a peacoat with a bright red pocket scarf folded sharply, his grey hair gelled back into a straight-lined parting. Oscar, his son from his third marriage – the house remembers his birth well, it happened in one of these very rooms – wanders out to the city at times, touring the bars and clubs with money to spare, though never a job to speak of. Over time, his options for places to get drunk have dwindled. His parents do not approve of his external pursuits, and the house has witnessed many arguments about it. They don't believe Oscar should be out in the city in his condition. But Tair House understands – Oscar has his own dark past that he's trying to push down deep, even if he doesn't remember it fully himself. It is no wonder he tries to drink away such sorrows.

Then there's Lucia, Xavier's third wife – a woman from a place no one has heard of, who wanders the house and its grounds dressed all in black with a funeral shroud over her face. When outside, which is rarely, she can be seen carrying an umbrella with a mahogany handle, as if she is allergic to the sun. Though, the house thinks, if she really was, then this would be the perfect place to be – this house, this city, where clouds gather obscuring all light.

Those who live near Tair House give it a wide berth. Visitors to the cemetery walk past it quickly, as if they don't notice it's there or that they're pretending it isn't. Maybe they are scared of this place. Maybe they're right to be. It is, after all, a house that can scare the clouds themselves from breaking.

In this city, where it rains

It was raining again, but it always rained in this city. The heavier the downpour, the stronger Maggie's ghosts came out, and tonight it was torrential.

Umbrella in hand, Maggie traversed the winding cobbled streets on her way home from her bar shift, dodging the spectral figures as she went. They stood here and there, hunched under streetlamps, or standing in the ever-constant puddles, bodies and faces distorted by the layers of rain. To most passers-by who denied the presence of the dead, they looked like a reflection or shadow. But Maggie had always been able to see them, especially on the dreariest of days, because ghosts are drawn to dreary things like rainclouds, cold empty streets, and sad young women.

When she was younger, and still getting used to her ghosts, Maggie would ask her gran who the rain people were. The ones with half melted faces, expressionless except for the occasional grimace. At first, not knowing any better, she would describe them in detail, even give some of the regular ones names – like Rose, the woman on West Street who stood outside the House with the Flowers, and Wallace, the boy that liked to sit on the Old Church Wall after dark. It was how she mapped the city – her own ghostly waypoints. West Street became Rose Way, and the crescent outside the church became Wallace's Smile. Her gran had at first entertained her descriptions of the strange figures she saw in the rain, though would look at her with a distant look in her eyes. Then she'd give a twisted smile as she said, 'you have such an imagination, Maggie,' then later, 'this needs to stop, Maggie, you're too old for this.' Now, she kept the knowledge of the ghosts to herself, the way they changed, the places they haunted, the corners they lingered in.

Outside, the ghosts didn't always stay in the same place, either – sometimes they moved, or gathered, and when the rain was heavy Maggie could even hear them. An echoing thrum of gathered spirits amongst the screams of rain. She could hear them now, though she wasn't in the mood to acknowledge them – it was late, and she was tired after a busy shift. She just wanted to get home, back to her flat where it was dry and warm, and where the ghosts receded to shadows lurking in the corners. Out of sight, mostly out of mind.

Now that she was older, Maggie barely flinched on passing them – even if they walked into or near her. They would simply disappear under her umbrella, melting into the dry. The ghosts, at least, had never been able to touch her.

*

When she arrived back at the terraced flat, her gran's cat Arlo greeted her with the same hungry mewing he always did, crying as if she hadn't left a full bowl of food and a heated blanket on before she headed out for her shift. After realising he wasn't getting fed this late, he ambled back through the thin crack in the door to her gran's room. Maggie pushed the door slightly more ajar, and peered in. Arlo had returned to his bed that sat on the shelf beside her gran's rocking chair, which was creaking slightly back and forth, cast in shadow.

'Sleep well,' Maggie said, before leaving them be. She knew her gran could never hear her, even if the routine of it made her feel less lonely in this grey city full of ghosts. Her gran wasn't as solid as the ones outside. She was just a shadow, stretched and amorphous, like a cloud above rain. Sometimes at night, Maggie heard the click-clack of her knitting needles. Other times, she heard her singing the same lullaby her mum often sang to her in her dreams, '*rain rain, go away, come again another day.*' And almost every time, she wanted to go in and tell her she had told her so, that ghosts were real, because here she was, dead, and still sitting in her chair, singing or knitting. Meanwhile, Maggie had been left to face her world of shadows all alone.

Smoke and Bitters

Maggie had been dreaming about her mum again. Her face was contorted in the dream, her expression rearranging with Maggie's distorted memories of her. Sometimes, she had turquoise eyes, sometimes a deep green. Sometimes there was a cut in her hairline, blood pouring down rosy cheeks that were lit only by a strange dim candlelight. And sometimes her face was as white as a sheet, and she'd smile down and hum a soft lullaby, her hand on Maggie's face. She knew it wasn't real, but she often found herself unable to wake, even when she realised what was happening.

During last night's dream, her mum had taken her face in her hands, held it so tight that Maggie could still feel the force of her grip when she eventually woke. She had come so close that Maggie could smell her lavender soap and feel the whisper of her breath against her cheek. The words she had last spoke rung in her ears now, as sharp and cold as her touch: *'Be careful, Maggie. Don't go back. Never go back.'* It wasn't the first time she'd said words in her dreams, even though Maggie could never make much sense of it. She couldn't remember anywhere she'd been before moving in with her gran after her mum had died when she was just six years old. She barely even remembered her mum, and often, she found herself wondering if the face in her dreams was one she'd made up. Her mum was the only ghost Maggie really wanted to appear in the rain, and she was the only one that never did.

*

Maggie arrived at her next shift feeling already tired. After the dream of her mother, she'd spent the day with a strange feeling, a coldness as if she'd been standing in the rain for too long.

The bar she worked in had once been a whisky distillery and was now furnished, complete with barrels stacked up at the sides or made into tables with wooden stools around them. It smelt of oak, varnish, and smoke, and candles on the tables and sconces on the walls were the only light source – Angus, the owner, kept things as old fashioned as the drinks.

Maggie liked the job because of the dark. In the underground space, the patrons were barely distinguishable from the ghosts and for a time, she could pretend like there weren't any shadows lurking here and there at all. Besides, Angus was kind, and he treated her well. And Maggie didn't really have any other friends in the city.

Her first customers were a group of tourists, with an accent she couldn't place. When she brought them a flight of whisky drams to taste, she asked them how long they were visiting for.

'What do you mean?' the man said picking up one of the glasses, sloshing it back and forth, watching it carefully as if trying to figure out its taste from look alone.

'You're tourists, right?'

'Ah, yes, just visiting,' another one of them said. 'Such a beautiful city.'

'Just a shame about the rain,' Maggie quipped.

'It's rained the whole time we've been here!' the first man said.

'And how long has that been?'

'Oh,' the man frowned, his mouth forming an 'o'. 'Well, how long have we been here?' he asked the woman to his left. But she didn't answer. Her face went blank for a long moment. Then she looked to Maggie. 'We're having a lovely trip, we decided to stay an extra day or two,' she said.

Maggie nodded slow. 'Oh, well. Enjoy the whisky, any questions, just shout,' she said, and left them. When she got back to the bar, Maggie had a strange feeling she'd seen them here before. Maybe they made repeat visits to the city. Except, they seemed to be acting like this was the first time they'd seen this place – wide-eyed, cautious. She watched them as they laughed and drank, then left before she could speak to them again. She didn't get to dwell on it for any longer, as a new customer arrived on his own. He hunkered down in a pokey table in the darkest corner. Despite this, and the fact he didn't seem to want to be noticed, she couldn't help but do just that. He was dressed shabbily, clothing holed, the fabric faded, but she could tell he was rich. There was a type of rich man she'd noticed that came to bars like this – the kind that liked to dress a little rough to hide where they came from. But Maggie could tell from how they held themselves that they were from a different world. Something in the way their shoulders tilted back, neck stiff, or how their eyes darted here and there, beady and watching. Distrustful. This man looked older than he probably was, wrinkles lining his eyes and forehead, as if he'd spent his entire life frowning. She steeled herself and approached the table, pad in hand.

'Welcome to The Undercroft,' she said, putting on her cheeriest of welcomes. 'What can I get you?'

'Grim name for a bar,' the man said in a posh Scottish accent, the kind that lilts and rises as if he was trying to hide that he came from anywhere at all. He looked around the walls and shivered. 'Where'd you get the name?'

'It's where the dead come to drink,' she said sardonically, her eye catching a movement in the corner just behind him. The man noticed her gaze and glanced behind, fixing for just a moment on the shadow.

But he turned back smiling. 'At least they must be unfussy customers.'

'What can I get you?' she repeated, not in the mood for a conversation with a guy like this.

'Surprise me.'

One of *those* customers. 'What sort of things do you like?'

'Hmm. I guess something smoky, maybe a little bitter, do you have anything like that?'

She smiled sweetly then made to head to the bar, but the man suddenly reached out to her to pull her back. 'Wait, do I know you?'

She tensed as his cold fingers gripped her arm, a sharp reminder of the way her mum had held her just the night before. Then, noticing her response, he retracted his hand straight away, and leaned back into shadow, a frown on his face. 'I'm...I'm sorry,' he said. 'I don't know why I did that. You just looked really familiar...that's all.' A look of alarm passed across his face, and she shook her head in a dismissive sort of way. She rubbed her arm where hairs had risen, then she turned back towards the bar, feeling the man's eyes on her back the whole time.

As she began to make the drink, a whisky cocktail with a dash of honey and orange bitters, Angus came across to check on her. He nodded towards the corner. 'He giving you bother?'

'It's okay. Nothing I can't handle.'

'Aye, I know,' he said. 'But if he does, you let me know. Looks like one of those rich types with more money than sense.'

She looked across at the man again, and found he was still looking at her, his candlelit eyes like dull flames in the dark. She dropped her gaze and looked back to Angus. 'Maybe he'll tip well.' She wondered what brought him to this dreary bar in the dregs of the city – most customers they had here were regulars, friends of Angus, or tourists who usually stopped by for a quick drink before heading to somewhere more exciting.

The man drank three whisky cocktails before moving onto the straight stuff – slow dram after slow dram. The bar soon emptied, and Angus started cleaning up in the back. The man had barely moved from the spot, sitting in the dark on his own, eyes narrowed in the dim light, staring at nothing in particular, leg tap-tapping rhythmically as if it was marking the seconds pass.

'Can I call you a taxi?' she asked him after the last order bell.

He blinked up at her, like he was surprised she was there. 'Oh. Is that my hint to leave?'

'Last call was half an hour ago,' she said, trying to keep the irritation from her voice.

He swilled the remaining dregs of the whisky in the glass. 'I'm still finishing my drink.'

'Maybe the bill then?' she suggested.

He let out a long sigh. 'Sure, yeah. You take cash?'

She shrugged. 'Of course.'

He leaned into his pocket taking out a wad of money, counting out two crisp £50 notes. He placed them on the table, stared at the paper for a few seconds with a frown. 'Does that cover it?'

'I'll get you some change.'

'No no, no need, no need. You keep it.'

She hesitated. 'That's almost double the cost of drinks.'

'For the service,' he said, looking around at the rest of the empty bar. Considering he'd drunk half the whisky bottle, and the cocktails before, he barely showed any hint of being intoxicated. 'Anyway, money doesn't exactly matter in this city anyway,' he said. 'But this place is great, you know.'

Maggie turned away, intent on getting him the change – she didn't like the idea of him thinking she needed it. Though when she brought it back and placed it down, he didn't lean for it.

'So, taxi?' she suggested again. 'I'll need an address?'

'I don't know where I'm going,' he said, unmoving.

She was starting to lose patience. 'I just need to close up. Angus will be back in here soon, and he won't be as patient as me,' she said, to remind him they weren't alone here.

His eyes tracked the room. 'I don't want to go home.'

'Well, that's not really my problem,' she said. 'Sorry.'

'I like it here,' he said, his voice suddenly low. 'It's quiet. Everywhere else in this city…it's just so loud, and crowded, and forgettable, and well, I just like it here.' He paused and looked up at her, something familiar in his gaze – a sadness in his eyes. 'But you're right, of course. Sorry for keeping you late, I don't want to be a bother, so I'll be on my way.' He stood, steady on his feet. 'Nothing worse than someone overstaying their welcome.'

She raised an eyebrow. 'Do you need a taxi called?'

He shook his head. 'I'll just walk for a while, I think.'

'This late?' she said, unsure why she was worrying about this man who clearly could afford to hail a taxi to wherever home was, if he needed it. But there was something about him that made him seem vulnerable. Like he might walk out into the street and disappear. She wondered if anyone would care enough to look for him.

'I like the dark,' he said, brushing it off. With that and a slight wave, and a final glance into the corner where Maggie had seen the shadowy ghost earlier, the man propped himself up with his mahogany-handled umbrella and left.

Maggie was still standing staring at the empty table when Angus came through from the back. 'You okay getting home tonight?' he asked. 'I could give you a lift back if you want?'

'That's okay, I'll get the night bus,' she said. 'Still running for another hour.'

Angus looked down at the money on the table. 'A good tipper after all,' he said, and when she picked it up to split it between them, he waved her away. 'Your table, your earnings. That's the rule. Wonder if he'll come back.'

Maggie couldn't decide whether or not she wanted to meet the man again.

*

As Maggie got off the night bus home, the rain was a soft drizzle. The lamps on her street were bright, and underneath one stood a familiar ghost. They could almost be human, if not for their melted expression and the way their limbs seemed to blend into their body. She tried not to look at them as she passed, even as they rasped a light whisper. It was the same muddled hiss they often made when she went by them. Maybe they were trying to tell her something. All these ghosts in this city with something to say, yet she was never able to really understand them. Sometimes she wished she could, that maybe their words would explain something of this curse. But mostly she was glad she couldn't hear them – the vision of the ghosts was enough to put up with every day, without having to know their thoughts, their personalities.

She walked quickly, umbrella in hand past the tall hedges of the colony flats to her right, down the cobbled street to her own building. And there was the Green Man, the one that lived perpetually trimming the hedge outside his old flat. He was one of the rare ghosts she did know when he was living, and his presence always slightly unnerved her because of that. Beside him, Arlo was sitting watching as the figure swayed back and forth in the rain.

'You want to come in?' she asked the cat, but he ignored her. He was unbothered by the rain, so she left him staring at the ghost. Apart from her, cats seemed to be the only other presence in the city that sensed the dead, and maybe the Green Man had been kind to Arlo once. She'd not known the man's name though her gran used to talk of the elderly man downstairs who helped her with the garden now and again. When he died, shortly after her gran had, and his daughter had come to clear out his flat, she'd not said anything to her. She felt bad about it, that maybe she should have told his daughter nice things about him helping her gran. But she worried that maybe the woman would move into his old house like Maggie had done with her gran's. Then they'd have to be neighbourly, with this shared experience, and she'd want to talk about her grandfather to her, all while he haunted the hedge outside. It would feel too awkward, and besides, she would rather stay anonymous. She didn't get to know her neighbours if she could help it. She didn't get to know anyone if she could help it. In case they died and became one of her ghosts.

She was passing by the Green Man to the entrance to her building, when suddenly he was looking at her. Or appeared to be looking at her. She held the umbrella firmly over her and made to keep walking, but as she did, he reached out all of a sudden. His hand melted under the protection of the umbrella and for a moment he stood there half-formed, his face rearranging with the rain. Then he spoke.

'Help. Me.'

Maggie froze. The ghosts never spoke like this. Never actual words. Maybe she'd misheard. Or maybe these had been his last words, a memory, an echo, and it was just by chance she happened to be here to see it. But then something grabbed her arm. As impossible as it was, she felt his grip on her wrist, cool fingers tight and strong. She tried to pull away and the Green Man fell forwards under her umbrella. His form melted beneath it, but she could still feel him, still feel his hand on her wrist.

'Get off me!' she shouted, starting to panic. 'Let go.'

By the edge, Arlo was hissing and snarling, hackles raised. He swiped at the air, letting out a low mewing sound.

Maggie pulled back again, and finally the Green Man released her. She fell into the pavement, landing hard. A sharp pain shot up from her hand. She'd landed on glass, and there was a sharp cut across her palm. She held it tight as warm blood mixed with rain, her umbrella fallen to the side. The Green Man stood over her almost solid now. Arlo was still letting out a low noise, ears pointed right back. She started to shake from the cold and shock. The ghost leaned towards her, inches from her face.

'Sorry,' he said in a strangled voice. His mouth gaped as he spoke, little cords of sinew stretching between where lips should be. 'I want to leave this place. I want to find my family. I thought you were one of us. I thought you could help.' Then, he straightened, and strode back to his hedge with his back to her as though nothing had happened. He began cutting away as he usually did with phantom shears, only a muffled whispering again that was almost lost in the sound of the rain.

Maggie stood up quickly, gathered her things and ran to her door, put the key in the lock and ushered Arlo in after her. He didn't need telling twice and shot straight up the stairs to the first floor flat. Her breath was hitching in her throat as she reached the landing, her keys bloodstained and rattling. With Arlo inside, he mewed at her for attention, but she had to clean her cut first. She took some kitchen towel to wipe away the blood then ran it under water to clean it. Hesitantly, she dried and looked at the damage. There was a small gash from below her thumb into the centre of her palm. It was long but not too deep, and she padded it with more kitchen towel and held her arm above her head.

Arlo was still crying at her, and she shushed him. He made another indignant sound, jumped up on her bookcase and watched her from a distance.

'You saw that too, right?' she asked him. 'The ghost—he grabbed me. That old man from downstairs. He actually held me, spoke to me. Said he…'

Arlo did nothing but glare at her.

'You must have known him, when gran lived here, didn't you?'

If he made any movement, it was in consternation rather than confirmation. Of course he didn't understand her. He could see the dead but understanding the living was one step too far. 'If you can understand me, meow twice?'

Arlo was silent. Maybe she'd lost more blood than she realised. She unpeeled the kitchen towel to examine her hand again. Thankfully the wound was no longer bleeding so profusely, though it had stained her white work shirt. She rolled up her bloody sleeves and paused.

'Maybe I'll have another scar,' she said, as if to Arlo. She had an unfinished half triangle shape on her forearm where she'd fallen down some stairs as a child and landed on a rusty banister. She couldn't remember it, but Gran had said she'd needed stitches. She thumbed the white lines absentmindedly and told herself if she coped with such an injury when she was so young then she could deal with a little cut on her palm. But it wasn't the cut that bothered her. It was the Green Man, and the way he'd grabbed her. Her mind buzzed with possibilities of it. This ghost had *touched* her. He'd spoken to her, seen her. Did that mean ghosts could properly hurt her, too? All these years, that had never felt like something she needed to worry about.

There was a creak from the other room: she'd almost forgotten about Gran. Hesitantly, she wandered to the second bedroom and slowly opened the door. The rocking chair was scraping back and forth, but her gran was only a shadow. She tiptoed over to her. Arlo wrapped around her ankles, purring softly. He was looking at the chair too, and as she got closer it stopped moving. A chill ran up Maggie's spine, hairs rising on the back of her neck.

'Gran, are you there? Can you hear me?'

There was no reply.

'Something is wrong,' she said. 'The Green Man, your neighbour from downstairs, he saw me.'

There was silence for a few long seconds, then Gran's chair began to rock again. Frustration built up and Maggie had a sudden idea. She went to the kitchen and filled up a large glass of water, then returned to the room. With a breath held, she threw the water at the chair.

The result was so sudden Maggie almost fell backwards again. Her gran's face, half-melted caught in the splash of water and hung in the air, disconnected from her body. The face looked at Maggie with dark dead eyes and a jaw half broken. Arlo meowed loudly, staring up between Maggie and the face, looking curious rather than fearful. Her gran's head hung like that in the centre of the room for several long seconds, staring at Maggie until the final remnants of the water dripped away and left her as just a shadow again. A moment later, the chair was creaking once more, and Arlo settled on his shelf to her side.

'S-sorry Gran,' she said, swallowing back tears. 'I shouldn't have done that.' *And I won't do it again*, she thought, wondering if the image of her gran's disembodied head would ever leave her mind. Maggie shuddered, left Arlo sitting there and pulled the door behind her.

In the living room, she peered out the window to the cobbled street below. The rain was torrential now and ghosts crowded along the cobbled street, wandering aimlessly up and down, faceless and grey. Then, as she watched, the ghosts all stopped. They turned towards her first-floor window and looked directly up at her. Heart hammering in her chest, she pulled the curtains shut and ran back to her living room.

That night, she didn't dream of her mother. Instead, she dreamed of a thousand ghosts reaching out to grab her, pulling her down into a dark grey abyss, all while she called out for someone to help her. But no help came.

Close encounters

After the night of the Green Man, Maggie stayed inside for two days. She called in sick to work, explained about her hand and that she couldn't carry drinks. Angus was understanding – she rarely took sick days – and it was early in the week so it wouldn't be too busy. But as the weekend approached, she knew she'd have to go outside again eventually, so, hesitantly, umbrella in hand, she left her flat.

The Green Man wasn't there by the hedge, but there were a few ghosts milling around. To her relief, none looked at her as she passed. She gave them a wide berth anyway, just to be safe. The rain was a light drizzle, the kind that stuck to solid things and got you more soaked than it should. But she was glad of it, because it meant the faces were less pronounced, and in the daylight, she could walk past them and pretend they were merely shadows or tricks at the corner of her eye. She picked up groceries in the corner shop near Wallace's Smile, avoiding Wallace, and the unnamed ghost that had a few months ago begun lurking by the postbox at the intersection. Then she went to the pharmacy as her hand had become sore and swollen. She asked the pharmacist for advice, and the woman inside took her round to the consulting room and cleaned the wound and gave it sticky stitches. 'You should have come in sooner,' she said, and Maggie tried not to look at her dual-shadow behind her, one of them moving in a distorted motion. 'But hopefully this will do it. If it swells up or you lose any feeling in your hand, best go to your GP or minor injuries.'

Maggie rolled her sleeve back down and noticed the woman's eyes track to her scar on her forearm – people couldn't help but look at it. The scar was so clean and sharp that it almost looked like she could have done it herself. But, as with anyone else who spotted it, the woman said nothing while Maggie avoided eye contact.

By the weekend, no ghosts had bothered her, and the swelling in her hand had gone down, so she made her way into work. Angus fussed over her when she arrived – he blamed himself for not giving her a lift home after dark.

'It probably would have happened anyway,' she told him. 'I'm just clumsy.'

He looked thoughtful for a moment, his thick black eyebrows knitting together in the way they often did when it seemed he wanted to ask her more. He always decided against it though, and sighed instead. 'Aye, you've broken a fair few glasses in your time here, more than the dayshift crew put together.'

'Not that you hold it against me or anything,' Maggie said with a smile.

'Well, you just take care tonight.' He said, then added, 'You would tell me if something was wrong, wouldn't you?'

Maggie sucked in a breath and forced a smile. 'Of course. I'm fine.'

Angus said a small, 'hmm', then continued polishing some glasses without another word.

She pulled the apron around her waist and looked around the bar – there were a couple of customers in the post-work slot, and she was about to head to get their order when she noticed the man in the corner again. She almost didn't see him – the candle on his table had burned out and he looked like one of her ghosts, hidden in the shadows. As she looked over, he caught her eye and waved her over. There was something in his expression that was oddly familiar, like she'd met him more than just the last time he was in the bar. She frowned and looked to Angus.

'Oh, he's been in every night this week,' Angus said. 'Pretty quiet, orders whisky and sits there till closing. Want me to get him?'

'No, that's okay, I'll go,' she said and wandered over to him with a new tealight. She lit it and placed in in the centre of the table.

'I hear you've become quite the regular,' she said.

'Uh, yeah I guess so,' he said, smiling up at her.

'What can I get you? Something bitter and smoky?'

'You remembered.' His face lit up. 'That would be perfect.'

'Won't be a minute.'

'Wait…Maggie is it?'

She turned. 'Angus told you my name?'

He shrugged. 'Heard him say it earlier. It's nice to meet you Maggie, I'm…' He stopped himself, then he glanced to the shelf display to his side where an array of bottles were arranged. 'Jack…' he said after a moment. 'I'm Jack.'

Maggie raised an eyebrow and looked to the shelf. The row of whisky bottles were mostly Scottish, but there was one Jack Daniels. Angus kept it in case, in his words, "tourists with no taste" came in.

'Jack,' she said, deciding not to pull him up on it. Was there a reason he didn't want her to know his real name? It made her more curious than she'd like to have admitted. 'Nice to meet you, *Jack*.'

'You know, it's the strangest thing,' he continued. 'I feel like we know each other.'

'Is that why you've been back every night?'

'Uh, yes, actually,' he said, shrinking in his chair. 'Oh god, that sounded less creepy in my head, I only meant…as I said last time, I like it here.'

Maggie flinched and she had half a mind to go tell Angus that she had a stalker and ask him to kick him out. But she couldn't avoid the fact that she felt the same way – like she knew him, that their paths had crossed before. Behind her, Jack's eyes kept glancing at an empty chair in the bar, and Maggie followed it to the presence that sat at the corner of it. Angus's brother, their most regular customer, now just a ghostly shadow.

'He looks…sad,' Jack said, his eyes still fixed on the chair.

Maggie spun round. 'What?'

Jack paused then coughed. 'Um. The bartender,' he said. 'He's just standing there…staring at that chair.'

'Oh,' Maggie said. 'Well, yes, that's where his brother used to sit.'

'And you knew him…the brother?'

She nodded. 'They owned this place together. He died.'

'This city is full of death,' he said, then, correcting himself. 'Sorry. I mean…how morbid of me. This isn't going well, is it? And I'm taking up too much of your time already.'

'I'll get your drink, Jack,' she said placing emphasis on his name.

He looked up at her blinking rapidly then he smiled. As she walked away, she heard him exhale loudly, before he began muttering something to himself, as soft and quiet as the ghosts in the rain.

'All good?' Angus asked her as she returned to make the drink.

'It's odd,' she said. 'He seems so…familiar. Like I've met him before, somehow.'

Angus's eyes narrowed. 'Maybe it was in another life.'

*

Maggie found herself checking on Jack more regularly during the evening than she usually would with customers. At a quiet point in the shift, Jack asked her where she was from. 'I'm trying to place your accent,' he added.

She shrugged. 'I've always lived here.'

He cocked his head slightly, then with a sigh said, 'Just like everyone else here.'

Maggie hadn't really thought about it before, but this wasn't the sort of city where you came and went. Her gran was from here, and she supposed her parents had been too, even if she couldn't really remember them. 'Where else is there?'

'Have you ever left the city?' he asked.

'Left?' She let out a slight laugh. 'To go where?'

'Anywhere!'

'I go to the beach, sometimes.'

'That's still part of the city,' he said, his jaw working silently. 'What do you do there?'

She shrugged. 'Sit and watch the waves mostly.'

'And there must be land across the sea, right?'

Maggie thought about the view from the beach – every time she'd looked out across the water a thick haar had settled in, so that she could only see a couple of meters in front of her. 'I don't know.'

'Have you ever tried to go further, than the city, than the beach, than the sea?'

'I don't know,' she said, her mind whirring. 'I mean, no, why would I want to?'

'Why wouldn't you want to?'

She shook her head, thoughts muddled in her mind. Why had she never thought about it before? Why hadn't she tried to go anywhere that wasn't this city? Wasn't this all there was? Gran never mentioned anything beyond it. But now that she thought about it, they had tourists, they had visitors, so where did they come from? Her head felt tight, stretched, as she grappled with the meaning of it. 'Have you been anywhere else?' she asked.

Jack was silent for a while before answering. 'No. Though, sometimes I'll go to the beach and stay underwater for as long as I can hold my breath. I'll swim and swim, because somehow my head feels clearer in water, like I can feel everything. I think that maybe I'll reach land. Maybe I'll get to somewhere that isn't here if I just swim for long enough. But then when I come above water, I've barely left the shore.'

Maggie shivered. She'd never liked swimming. The ghosts were more solid in water, faces formed into strange expressions, usually with mouths gaping wide as if caught in a forever drowning. Once, when she was little, she saw a ghost lying on the seabed looking up at the fog-filled sky above, and when they opened their mouth, a crab crawled out of it. Now, if she visited the beach, she only ever dipped her toes in. 'Maybe it's the sea currents, Gran always told me the tides were strong in the city.'

'Maybe that's all it is,' he said quietly. 'But if you've been here since you were little, then what year is it?'

She frowned. 'What do you mean?'

'The year,' he said. 'Time has passed, but what year is it? How many years have you been in this city, and only this city?'

She tried thinking about it, tried putting a number together in her mind, but anytime the numbers formed, they blurred and separated. And now there was a piercing ringing in her ears. 'The city is all I've ever known.'

Jack nodded slow, the corner of his mouth curling downwards. 'I've read about there being a whole other world, in the books we have at home,' he said. 'They're not like the books in the city, the ones with blurred pages, and broken paragraphs, the ones hiding the truth. Maybe the rain is washing it all away.' He was speaking in riddles now. 'But we can never leave, we can never reach anywhere that's not here.'

Maggie didn't understand, and as she stared at him, for a moment she felt like she was staring through him. She sucked in a breath and blinked awake, pushing past the ache building across her temple. 'Can I get you another drink?'

He sighed. 'Um, sure. Do you have anything without whisky?'

Maggie gestured to the room around, the signs, displays, and barrels, and Jack smiled. 'Another whisky it is then. I guess it is the water of life. It'll probably do me some good.'

Maggie left the conversation feeling uneasy. Like there'd been more left unsaid between them. Why had Maggie never left the city? Her gran had barely even taken her beyond their neighbourhood growing up, and the only memory of visiting somewhere different was of an old house. There was one memory in particular, and it came in a flash back to her now.

She was running up and down a grand staircase, laughing as she played hide and seek with her mum. Then, when her mum found her, she chased her all the way from the landing and out into the grounds, where they spent the afternoon collecting brambles and watching the birds. That house must have been where she'd lived before. Maggie only had a single photograph from back when she was a toddler, from when her mum was still alive – she was sitting on that same stair with her mum, her dark brown curly hair that Maggie had inherited reaching past her shoulders. Maggie was looking up at her face with a smile, and her mum was smiling too even if it didn't reach her eyes. There were no photos of her with her dad, though Gran kept some around the flat of him from when he was younger – before her parents had met. He'd died suddenly at home, just after she was born, and she'd never really known him. Her gran had always said Maggie was the only part of him that she had left, but she never talked about what had happened to him. Over the years Maggie had learned not to ask. Her gran had never suggested going back to where she'd spent her first years, and Maggie had never really wanted to. That was where her parents had died, along with most of her memories of them. Now that her gran was gone, she'd probably never get a chance to know what her past held.

*

The rest of her shift went smoothly, and it was quiet for a Friday night. A couple of times, she caught Jack looking at the bar, directly at where the shadow of Angus's brother sat.

Maggie told herself he was probably just deep in his thoughts. She'd never met anyone else who could see the ghosts, despite hoping she would for a long time, so why would that change now?

Before last orders, Jack stood up, gave a slight nod over to the bar and left without a word. Maggie wondered if she'd see him again.

'Who do you think he really is?' she asked Angus as they cleaned the tables and tidied away the chairs for the night. Maggie reset each of the candles one by one, ignoring the shadows in the corner as she always did.

'Who, that posh lad that drinks alone and likes you by the looks of it?'

Maggie shrugged. 'He just seems…different.'

'I'd be careful, he's got a strange look in his eye,' Angus said. 'Though, he's become our best customer over the past week. Never seen anyone able to drink like that. He'd put my brother to the test.' Angus looked fondly at the empty chair and tapped the counter in front of it.

'Yeah, and he always tips well,' Maggie reasoned.

'Aye, all about the service,' he said, with a glimmer in his eye. 'That why you wonder who he is? Have a mind to get to know him better?'

Maggie focussed on polishing a glass more than it probably needed. She'd never got to know anyone – never had a friend in the city, apart from Gran, Arlo, and Angus. But Jack…he was mysterious. Interesting, even. And part of her did want to figure out who he was. 'Hmm,' she said to Angus. 'Maybe I do.'

The House

Tair House watches the city as it sleeps, almost envious as the rain pours endlessly. Meanwhile, grey clouds gather and never break above the crumbling walls, shading the darkness within. Or, never letting it out. It is no wonder plants can barely survive in the grounds here – the sun fights and fails to break through, and any trees that do survive the lack of light, must pull the water in from the air, or stretch their roots far enough beyond the house's boundaries to steal water from the city itself. The city, the house thinks, has plenty to spare.

It must have rained here once, but the house cannot remember. It remembers lots of things – some of them good, some of them bad, but many of them woven with moments of sorrow and pain. There has been death here, so much that the house wonders if that is why it can feel itself dying. Why it can feel its very foundations sinking, or its walls crumbling piece by piece. Those that are living in the house must be able to feel it too – the gradual death of their family home. The dead can certainly feel it – they tell the house every day of the way they feel stretched, lost, pulled into a growing darkness. Sometimes, the house wishes it could rip up its roots and walk into the city. Plant itself somewhere under rainclouds that break, and skies that are open. Become a normal house in a place less haunted.

Sometimes, the house wishes it were truly alive, not trapped between this dark inbetween of life and death. A house, it is said, is much like those who call it their home.

Ghosts in the rain

Jack didn't return the following day, nor during the week after, and Maggie found herself looking up every time the door to the bar opened, or when she heard the tip tap of an umbrella against the old stairs. But Jack never came.

It was when she was walking home in the rain that she saw him next. He was standing on the corner of Rose Way, looking up at the House of the Flowers, and, directly at the ghost standing outside it. He was standing without an umbrella this time, soaked to the skin, making his clothes look distorted and dull. Next to Rose on the path she could hardly tell which one of them was a ghost.

'Jack?' She ambled over, aware of the darkness surrounding them. 'You'll catch a death in this rain.'

He turned to her, clearly surprised to see her. 'Oh, Maggie? Hello.'

'Why are you just standing here?' she said, then had the sudden realisation that the streets were quiet, and maybe he knew she might come this way to walk home. Maybe he was here because of her. Her neck prickled with unease, and she held the umbrella firm, ready to use it as a weapon if needed. But Jack didn't look threatening. He was still staring at Rose and the House of the Flowers.

'It's an interesting house,' she said, pointing at the gate. Rose bushes crept all the way from the gate to the walls, their bright colour contrasted against the dilapidated building behind.

'She must have loved this house, to stay here,' Jack said, almost to himself, then he spun and looked at Maggie. 'I mean…'

'You can see her?' she said, before she could stop herself.

He didn't reply, only stared at her with his wide grey eyes, though now that she noticed them they were more silver, gleaming like tiny five-pence coins.

'The woman…I call her Rose,' Maggie said, feeling a sensation she'd not felt in a long time. Excitement? Hope? Had she finally met someone like her? 'She's a ghost, I think.'

Jack stared at her for a long time, his expression almost unreadable. Then he stepped closer to her. His hair was rain-soaked and it looked like tangled vines as it stuck to his cheeks. 'I thought I was the only one like this,' he said.

'Me too.'

They stood there for a long time looking at one another, barely moving as if they were ghosts themselves. 'Would you…' she paused, not wanting to come on too keen. But she'd never met anyone who could see things the way she did. 'I mean, maybe we could get a drink, talk about it?'

The smile on his face was a distant one, mixed with a hesitation she couldn't place. 'Yes, definitely. I'd like that.' He looked up and down the street. 'Where's open?'

Maggie checked her phone. It was late – most bars would be closing up soon. 'Well, I have a day off tomorrow. Maybe we could meet somewhere for coffee?'

His expression dropped, a moment of disappointment, but then he nodded with a slight smile. 'Sure, that would be nice. There's a place in the old town, near the water. No ghosts inside,' he said. 'And it's quiet, no one will bother us.'

'Sounds perfect,' she said. 'Can you text me the address?'

He frowned. 'Oh, I don't own a phone.'

'What…why?'

He shrugged. 'I've never had anyone to message.'

Maggie felt another tug of a shared experience. Her entire phone storage consisted of the bar's number and pictures of Arlo. Now that she thought about it, she wondered why she even bothered with it at all. It's not like she had anyone to share the photos with. She pocketed her phone, then fumbled in her bag to find the crumpled city bus route map. 'Can you show me on here, then?'

He nodded and traced his finger along a route towards the waterway and down into the older part of town. 'See this the crescent shape before that side street,' he said. 'Dunedin Brews, is at the corner there. It's a nice place.'

'Great,' Maggie said. She called that street Dolly's Close – there was a ghost there that stood humming to herself in the road, staring wistfully in at a house with ceramic dolls in the window. 'I'll meet you there then.'

'Noon?' he said, taking out a pocketwatch of all things.

'Perfect,' she said, then she made to leave. 'Are you okay, staying here?'

He smiled. 'Yes, oh I'll probably head back home tonight. My parents will likely be wondering where I've been.'

'You still live with your parents?'

He shuffled awkwardly. 'Um, yes.'

'But aren't you rich?'

'I…I suppose, in a way.'

Maggie caught the pained look in his eye and decided not to press further now. She'd have plenty of opportunity to find out more about him tomorrow. With a buzz of excitement she'd not felt in a long time, she left Jack standing in the rain, and headed home for the night.

*

Maggie half expected Jack not to show up when she arrived at the small coffee shop the next day. It was hidden away along a side street and was similarly quirky to The Undercroft. An old sign stood outside the door that read *Dunedin Brews*, and the old brass door bell jingled as she opened it. She set her umbrella by the holder at the entrance and nodded to the woman at the counter. She smiled and ushered her towards a table near a woodburning stove and a bookshelf filled with old books. She scanned the spines of them while she waited.

She'd nearly not come. Meeting an almost-stranger in a coffee shop on her own wasn't her usual haunt. She'd not have the excuse of work, or a table to clean if the conversation got awkward. She tugged anxiously at her sleeves, and picked up a book just to look at, though she didn't register any of the words. It was a tourist book of the city, and it featured a drawing of the central castle with a blue sky above it. She frowned, touching the clear sky and trying to remember the last time it wasn't raining. She couldn't. Even the words on the book looked jumbled, like they were describing an entirely different city, not the one she knew, lived, and breathed.

The doorbell jingled again, and she put the book back quickly, before peering round the corner. She caught Jack's eye as he sauntered over. He'd dressed slightly less unkempt than usual, and he was wearing a long grey coat that was dappled with rain droplets. He'd remembered an umbrella this time which he placed next to hers.

'Hey.'

'Hey,' she replied.

The woman came over to take their order and they ordered black coffees with a croissant each. When it arrived, Maggie sipped at the coffee but didn't touch the pastry.

'So…' Maggie began.

Jack smiled and itched the back of his neck.

'No ghosts here,' Maggie said to break the silence. 'It's nice. Peaceful, I mean.'

'Right?' he said, pulling a layer off his croissant. 'That's why I chose it, really. I thought you'd like it.'

'Yeah, I do,' she said.

'Great.'

Maggie took another sip of coffee. 'So…how do we start this?'

Jack leaned back a little. 'I don't know. I mean, you could tell me when you started to see them. The ghosts, I mean.'

She nodded. 'I've always been able to, or at least I have for as long as I can remember,' she said, thinking of the picture with her mother, smiling up at her. Had she been able to see them then? 'How about you?'

'Yes, same,' he said. 'They've become more solid over the years though. I used to not be able to make out their features and then I started to see them more clearly as I…as I got older.'

'I only see them clearly in the rain,' she said.

'Yes, in water. They're much more complete there, but I

can see them inside too. Like the one at the bar your boss was looking at.'

'Angus's brother?'

'You see him there too?'

'Kind of. Though when I'm inside, without the rain, they're just a shadow for me.'

'Hmm,' he said. 'I wonder if…' He stopped himself and leaned back, frowning.

'What?'

He stared at her for a long moment, then his tone changed slightly as he asked, 'Can your family see them?'

Maggie shook her head. 'I don't know. My gran couldn't. She didn't even believe that I could, or at least if she did, she pretended she didn't. She brought me up, and I never really knew my parents.'

'Oh,' he said. 'I'm sorry.'

'I always wondered if one of them could see like me, but my gran eventually stopped answering any questions about it, and so I just accepted maybe I'd never know.'

'That must be hard,' he said. 'Not understanding where you're from. Sometimes I feel that way too.'

'But you know your family right, if you live with your parents?' Maggie said. 'Can they see the ghosts?'

He took a deep breath. 'In a way, maybe. Not in the same way as me. My mother, she…she's different. And my father, he's got other things on his mind. They don't like to talk about it much. They mostly just keep to themselves, at home.'

Maggie sat forwards. Could her ability have been passed on through her family? Maybe her mum *had* been able to see the ghosts as well. 'One of the ghosts grabbed me the other day,' she said out loud for the first time since. 'He even spoke to me.'

Jack stared at her, and Maggie couldn't tell whether he was surprised, worried, or a mix of the two.

'Has that happened to you?' she pushed.

He didn't answer straight away. 'I…well, not in the city.'

'I thought you hadn't left the city?'

'I just mean, there are ghosts where I live, in the house, my parents' house, and some of them are more…animated than others.'

'And you grew up there?'

He nodded. 'I was born there.'

'What's it like?'

'Old. Grey. Cold.'

'Like the rest of the city?'

'Sort of. But not quite,' he said. 'It's hard to explain without seeing it, but it just has its own sort of energy, if that makes sense. It's a historical building I guess, Tair House, have you heard of it?'

'I don't think so. Maybe you could give me a tour some time, then,' she said, realising as soon as she'd said the words it was probably too presumptuous.

But he just shook his head. 'Oh, I'm not sure that would be possible. It's all a bit complicated, with my family.'

Maggie was about to push further when the door to the café swung open and a tall man strode in. He didn't greet the owner, and instead swept across to their table and stared at them.

'So this is where you've been out galivanting to?' the man said to Jack, without so much as a glance to Maggie.

Jack stood up so quickly he spilled half his coffee out the mug. As Maggie wiped it up with a napkin, she noticed that Jack had even taken a little step away from the man. 'Is everything okay?' she asked, and the old man's eyes darted very briefly down to her.

'Sorry, um…this is my dad,' Jack said.

'I'm glad you remember, because your mother and I have been worried sick about you. You know fine well you're not supposed to be out and about as much as this. You've not even slept in your bed these past days, is this who you've been with.' The man gave Maggie another look but this time lingered a while, long enough to make Maggie uncomfortable and look away.

'This is Maggie,' Jack said. 'She's a friend. We're just having coffee.'

'Maggie?' the man's lip curled, and he looked her up and down again. Maggie did the same, noticing the old-fashioned clothes he was wearing. A peacoat, tweed trousers, a folded red pocket square.

'Dad, what are you doing here?'

'I came to bring you home.'

'How did you even find me?'

'I followed you,' he said. 'Heard you leaving the house this morning and drove behind you. Forgot how horrible this city is for parking, otherwise I'd have been here sooner, but here I am now. The car's nearby, time to go. We've not got long, and your mother is waiting.'

'No,' Jack said. 'I'm a grown adult, I can make my own decisions. I'm staying here to have a coffee with Maggie.'

His dad's attention moved to Maggie with a leering expression. 'And where did you two meet exactly?'

'At a bar,' Jack said.

'Where I work,' Maggie clarified.

'I see. Well, you'd do well to stop serving him. What's the name of your establishment?'

'It's not mine, I just work there,' she said, then to his silence added. 'It's called The Undercroft.'

'How morbid.' His lip curled, then he turned to Jack. 'But you need to stop going there, son, you know you can't spend too long away from the house. Not in your state.' Was that a hint of concern in his voice?

'What state?' Maggie asked.

His dad began to answer, but Jack cut in. 'I'm dying. Apparently.'

'Oh.' Maggie felt suddenly cold. 'I'm…I didn't realise. I'm sorry.'

Jack shook his head and gave her a slight shrug. 'It's fine, it's not a big deal. I've come to terms with it.'

His father bristled. 'Well all this drinking at bars into the small hours isn't helping. All you're doing is worrying your mother sick, and you know how she gets.'

Jack shook his head, shoulders slumped. 'Sorry about this,' he said to Maggie, eyes to the floor. 'I should really go.'

But she put her hand on his arm. 'Jack, you don't need to.'

'*Jack*? Oh lying now, are we?' his father sneered. 'Are you so ashamed of our family you would hide your own name?'

'You can't speak to me like that, I'm not a child anymore.'

'Then stop acting like one *Oscar*.'

Jack—*Oscar* turned to Maggie with a pained look, then, resigned, began to leave the coffee shop. But his dad was looking at Maggie now, his eyes narrowed, making his cheekbones look even sharper. Then he stepped towards her, so close that she could smell his stale dank breath.

'It was nice to meet you. Maggie,' he said holding out a hand. She took it out of instinct, and he gripped it tight. 'Maggie…would that be short for anything by chance?'

'Yes. Margaret,' she said. 'But I go by Maggie. And you are?'

'Xavier,' he said. 'Xavier Logan.'

There was something strange in his eyes. As if he was trying to see through her, to read her mind. She couldn't shake the feeling she'd seen that look before. She tried to pull her hand away, but he held it tight, and she was reminded of the Green Man, of his pleas for help. 'Can I help you with anything else?' she asked.

'I know you,' he said, his voice suddenly low. 'We've met before.'

It wasn't in the tone of a question, and she glanced to Oscar. Though he seemed just as confused as she was.

'Where are you from?' Xavier pressed.

Maggie held her ground and his gaze, and there was that familiar look again – or had she only seen it in Oscar's eyes? The same silvery shade. 'I'm from here.'

'Yes, but *where*, exactly. The city is a big and sprawling place, *Margaret*.' There was a hunger in the way he said her name, like each syllable was a challenge.

'I'm not telling you where,' she said, noticing the wavering in her voice. There was something really wrong about this man, something that set an unease stirring in the pit of her stomach. She'd have happily run out of this coffee shop there and then if not for Oscar, who was frozen to the spot, watching helplessly. The confidence she'd seen in him in The Undercroft had evaporated as suddenly as the ghosts in the dry.

'Your family, what's your family name?' Xavier pressed on.

'You can't just demand information like that,' she said summoning some assertiveness back into her words. 'Now, let go of my hand. Please.'

Xavier didn't let go. His grip only tightened so that her fingers began to ache. She bit down on her lip so she wouldn't wince. His eyes moved down to her wrist, to the sleeve that had started to ride up revealing the base of the scar on her forearm. His mouth quirked, but before he could say another word, Oscar stepped in between them and pulled his father away. Xavier blinked rapidly as he let go of her hand, then he composed his face into something more neutral. He tensed his fists and his jaw as if it was her, not him, who'd locked their hands in a death grip. 'Maggie…Margaret…The Undercroft… interesting.' Then, after giving her a final look up and down, his gaze lingering again on her arm, he left as quickly as he had walked in.

'I'm sorry. I should go.'

'Jack…I mean Oscar, you don't need to,' she called out to him, but he had already picked up his umbrella. With an apologetic wave he was gone.

Maggie sunk down into the armchair and picked at the edges of her pastry. She felt cold. She wondered if she'd ever see him again – the man she'd briefly known as Jack. Oscar, completely changed under his father's control. And he was dying, too. Was that why he could see the ghosts? Did that mean she was dying too? But he'd always been able to see ghosts, and so had his family. And there was another question that niggled in her mind as she could still feel the grip of Xavier's hand on hers. Just like Oscar, she was sure she'd met him before.

The House

The house cannot exactly remember how it came to wake, but it has heard the tale many times on quiet and lonely nights, told through the cracks in its walls, words creeping in with the cold and dark, until this tale has become almost like a memory itself.

It starts with a man, so young and carefree that he had the dreams of a boy. As with the foolishness of youth, the boy fell in love with a girl. It is a common story, but this isn't quite that story.

In this tale, both boy and girl were obsessed with death and the occult. Together they travelled up and down the country, learning, and exploring, delving into strange lore, and visiting places with the darkest tales and most haunted locales. They met with academics, spirtualists, mediums, practicing witches, and anyone with a curiosity in the macabre and strange. Through their research, they learned to commune with the dead, to delve into the spirit realm, to break that boundary between life and other. Once they'd perfected their craft, they started performing their shows. Their magic and illusions became renowned to those in the know, and soon they were being invited to every wealthy house and estate across the country to showcase their affinity with the spirit world, to test the bounds between life and death itself. Until it came to be they arrived in this city, before it was a place of perpetual rain. The couple loved the city.

The way the sun illuminated even the greyest of buildings, the way the smell of the sea drifted in from the shore on a clear day, or how the tangy scent of the brewery every few days clung to your nose and didn't let go, so that the memory of it stayed with you. They liked the way the gardens bloomed with flowers, and trees grew tall in the parks, reaching for the sunlit sky. Everything was special about the city – the cobbled streets and layered buildings that towered high upon golden hills. And of course, its dark history, dozens of stories to tell and retell. Places to find. Mysteries to uncover. This, they thought, they would make their new home for a time. Though, perhaps, they did not quite expect the hold that this city and this house would soon have on them.

Together, the young couple prepared for an exclusive show at Tair House. Back then, the house was grand and impressive, nestled in a quiet dip, where the city's wildlife took refuge, and flowers bloomed in warm springs and summers. The owners had arranged an exclusive audience of the city's most elite in the house, and the guests arrived in pairs, dressed in the finest of dramatic garbs – red and black cloaks with hoods – matching the strange extravagance of the inside of the house itself. In the drawing room, the pair set up their usual ritual. First, they gathered the guests into a circle to bind an enchantment, then they instructed everyone to hold hands. The young man stood in the middle as the young woman lay down on the ground. She flashed a smile at the one she loved, would always love, hands rested gently across her belly, ready for the ritual. It was time to begin the commune with the dead, with the otherworld. For many years, the couple had touched the afterlife, had grown closer with the spirits. And here, in this house, came the next show of strength. They would open a gap to the other side, and communicate with those that came through.

Ignoring the gasps of the audience in the circle around them, the man knelt by his protégé's side and painted a mark on her arm with red ink — two partial triangles, one upside down, intersecting. A hexagram he'd seen in a grimoire on his travels. Something to bind the magic. Symbolic of blood, and a sacrifice intended. As she lay in the centre of the circle, body rested and eyes closed, he whispered softly to her. She soon fell into a trance. There was a hushed silence in the room, not even a whisper of wind from outside. Then, the woman screamed, eyes wide open. The young man knew from the surge of energy in the room that the ritual had succeeded. The young woman stopped screaming but remained in her trance as her partner continued and ordered the group to keep their circle. To await the spirits to visit. Soon, the commune would begin. And the house, now, remembers how it felt. How a new energy pulsed through it, as if the walls themselves were breathing, expanding all around it. Tair House was a part of the tale now, a part of the proceedings.

A tense silence fell across the room as the house watched the scene unfold. And then a voice came from the corner of the room, a whimper of a young girl. The girl was known to the house — she had grown up here, had laughed, cried, learned to walk, talk, and to sing sweet songs to any who would listen. She looked to the gathered group — the young couple in the centre, and the rich audience all dressed in their grandiose and strange costumes, faces concealed by shadows — and she started to scream. It was almost harmonised with a sudden shriek of the woman in the circle. The spirits, too, had begun to wake, and they were trying to take hold, trying to communicate with those in the room. The house awaited their arrival eagerly. But then, the man of the house, the father of the little girl left the ritual and rushed to pick up his screaming daughter and take her away. That was when it happened.

The circle broke.

All the lamps in the room snuffed out, leaving a dim light only from the candles on the side tables. In the clatter, the guests were caught in a panic, their imaginations getting out of hand. The house watched on, breathing in the scent of perfume and candle smoke, feeling suddenly hungry, powerful, and alive, all at once. Awake.

The young man tried to calm the gathered guests, to summon them back to his ritual. It was dangerous to break a bond to the other side in the middle of the summons, in the middle of a blood ritual, no less. Then his eyes tracked to his fearless assistant, the woman he loved — she was writhing on the floor, eyes wide but with an expressionless silvery stare. And as he watched on in horror, a clatter came from behind followed by a whorl of heat and smoke. Someone had knocked over a candlestick and set the tablecloth aflame. The gathered guests fled while the fire flared.

The house learned to breathe then, as the flames flickered across its walls. Its awareness spread into every room, above and below, even to the grounds outside, and the grand old ash tree that stood stalwart guarding the house itself.

The young man barely made it out of the house alive, carrying his beloved limp in his arms.

The man of the house stood outside, with his crying daughter wrapped around his neck, watching their home burn. Then his attention turned to the young couple he'd invited in.

He blamed them, not the little girl, for interrupting the ritual, nor those who had started the fire. So, the man of the house yelled at the young man, even as he cried for his beloved, begging her to wake. No one cared about her. No one called for help. She melted away into nothingness, her thoughts bleeding into the walls of the house itself.

The flames were eventually quelled but the damage was done. While the house would still stand, for the young man, it was too late. His beloved and the love she carried was no longer here. She had succumbed to the otherworld. She was gone, or at least, gone from his world. The house could still feel her though.

Years later, the young man returned to the house and begged the owner to let him back inside to finish the ritual he'd once started, in the hope it would bring the young woman back from the dead. He even warned the owner of what might befall him and the house if he didn't, but he was chased from the premises under threat of charges pressed. Arson, he claimed, even though the fire was all the fault of his scared little daughter. The daughter that still lived protected by these walls. For now, at least. For the house too had started to blame the young girl for breaking the ritual, for stopping the house reaching its full potential. One day, she would pay for what had happened, as would the man of the house. But it would take time, the house would have to be patient. It would have to wait until it was strong enough.

The young man's last words as he looked up at the old grey building, crevices beginning to appear in the walls and the roof, were 'I hope you all rot in this house.' Then he disappeared into the night.

The family of the house remained for some time, but tragedy quickly befell those who lived there. The couple who had owned the house died from a long sickness. When their young daughter, the girl at the start of it all, grew up and was married, and had a family of her own, they too were plagued by the same tragedy.

And now the new owners are facing a similar fate. One that traces back to the fateful day itself, of a girl crying, a woman dying, and a circle too long left broken.

The Letter

Maggie dreamt of her mother again. This time Maggie was trapped inside the walls of a house. A house that felt distant and familiar all at once. In the centre of a grand room her mother lay splayed out on the floor while Maggie cried and screamed out for her. Then, a shadow was creeping along the floor, ghost hands reaching up from the gaps in the wooden boards. The bodies then emerged, solidified, eyes empty, mouths wide, black blood spilling down their cheeks and chins. They folded forwards, engulfing her mother in a darkness that moved like a flutter of a thousand wings. Maggie cried out, tried to rip the walls apart to get closer, to save her, but her mum was gone, and she was left alone, trapped, until the ghosts turned, and came for her too.

She woke up to find Arlo sitting on her chest. He was staring at her with bright hazel eyes, and when she opened her own eyes, he pawed gently at her cheeks.

'Good morning to you too, Arlo.'

She looked to the curtains where a soft light was creeping in. Rain thrashed against her window in a drumbeat thrum. She lifted Arlo gently away, and he stretched out on the bed, able to make as many distorted shapes as the ghosts did. She got up but didn't open the curtains. Arlo was still watching her closely, as if he was concerned she might disappear.

After making herself a coffee, she got dressed, grabbed her raincoat and an umbrella, and headed out. It was her day off from the bar, and she always took a walk around the city on her day off. She walked up and down cobbled streets, stopped for another coffee, and browsed a second-hand bookshop full of old tomes, without buying anything. But she couldn't get the image of the man from yesterday out of her head. Xavier Logan – who was he? And why did he look so familiar. Maybe he was famous in some way, or she'd seen his picture in a book. She kept walking aimlessly, ignoring her ghosts, and the commuters so that they basically merged together in the rain. Then, as she passed the city records office she paused. Xavier seemed like an important man, rich at the very least. Maybe there'd be information about him somewhere, or even about Tair House – Oscar had mentioned it was a historic building. Before she could talk herself out of it, she went inside, leaving her umbrella at the door. The woman at the reception looked confused as she checked in.

'Hello there,' she said. 'Can I help you?'

'I'm hoping to do some research,' she said.

'Going to need more than that, love,' she said, not unkindly.

'I'm looking for information on a building in the city. Tair House. And a person. Xavier Logan.' Then at the woman's blank expression, added, 'for a project.'

'Looking up a new boyfriend or something?' she said, leaning over the desk, then she laughed. 'Just messing with you, I've not had many in today. Must be the rain, keeps folks at home and all that.'

'Ah, yeah, maybe,' Maggie said, offering an awkward smile.

'Well, I can give you a visitor pass, seen as it's quiet,' she said, ruffling with some papers under the reception desk. She handed the paper slip to her, though the name and date were blank. 'You can use the computers at the back to search for what you need in the digital archives, just use the keyword search. You can access whatever we have scanned in on the system, or you can look through the newspaper arhives physically but that will take a bit more time.'

'Thank you,' she said, feeling suddenly overwhelmed. But she took the pass still, and headed towards the computers. The one she sat down to was slow to open, the keyboard dusty. She searched for Tair House first in the digital archives and a list of items popped up. She clicked on the first one and scrolled down the article. The house was set within large grounds with a cemetery just beside it. She tried to find photos of it from recently, but the only ones available were blurry black and white historical ones, a grand house surrounded by pristine grounds. One article suggested that the house now lay empty – maybe the Logans travelled often, or maybe that was before Oscar became sick. Though Oscar wasn't mentioned in any of the information she found. Next she searched for any records on Xavier, and was surprised to find him pop up in several old articles. It seemed he'd been an occultist as a younger man, a famous one at that. She looked through the old pictures from scanned-in newspaper reports, some from events, interviews, reports of his performances, hardly able to believe the handsome smiling man was the one she'd met in the coffee shop. In one picture, there was a beautiful woman dressed in a black evening gown with him, named only as the Fearless Ferrante, his medium's assistant. She couldn't find anything on her, though Maggie thought she looked similar to Oscar, the same dark hair and sharp features. Was that his mother?

She was tempted to walk across town to see the house now, to speak to Oscar again, but when she looked outside she saw it was already getting dark. So, she shut down the computer, thanked the woman at reception, then headed home. The rain was torrential, and the ghosts were out in force, and by the time she got home she was drenched to the skin and freezing cold. She ran a bath to warm up, fed an annoyed Arlo – she hadn't meant to leave him all day – then checked on her gran. While in the room, she found herself picking up the photo of her and her mum on the counter. She looked closely at her mum's face – wondered again if it was familial, her ability to see ghosts. If her gran couldn't see it, then it probably wouldn't have come from her dad's side. Looking closely, Maggie found there was a distant expression in her mum's eyes in the photo. She was looking beyond the photo, and Maggie noticed for the first time the slight shadow across the wall. Could her mother see a ghost behind the frame, or was she just tired, sad. She was recently widowed, after all. Sadness followed Maggie's family around, it seemed.

Her mum died a few years after the photo was taken – that's why there was no real grave to visit, only a memorial that her gran had placed on a bench near one of the city's many parks. When asked what had happened to the place Maggie had lived before, her gran said it was gone too, along with everything her mum's family had owned before. Once, her gran had told her it was 'for the best,' and that she wouldn't have wanted to grow up there anyway, though Maggie had never found out why. Her gran kept secrets like they were treasure, locked away for safekeeping. Maybe there was a key to them somewhere.

*

That night Maggie arrived early for her shift having taken a taxi to avoid the rain. There was a small stream of water running down the stairs to the bar and she expected they'd be quiet tonight. Angus was waiting for her inside with a strange expression. He was holding an envelope, and he passed it over to her without a word.

She hesitated – tips had been split already this week, and she wasn't due another pay until Friday. Was Angus about to give her a notice to leave? She had been a bit distracted lately, with "Jack" and her hand injury. 'Did I do something wrong?'

He saw the look in her eyes and waved his hand. 'Oh no, no, it's not from me, don't panic. An odd-looking guy dropped this off for you.'

Maggie looked down at the envelope, thumbed the address which simply read *Margaret Fall*, no address. Her stomach dropped. *Margaret*. No one called her that. Not since yesterday when Xavier had asked about her. 'Did he leave a name?'

Angus shook his head.

'What did he look like?'

'Old, wore a ridiculous peacoat, looked all peely wally. Demanded I give this to you without even stopping to order a drink. He was…on edge to tell you the truth. Kept looking behind him, staring at the walls. You in some sort of trouble?'

Maggie's stomach twisted. 'No…no trouble, just…well, you know Jack?'

'The guy that drinks here when you're on shift?'

She gave a quick nod. 'Yes, well, he's actually Oscar, and this guy, I think he's his dad. I went for a coffee with Jack – I mean Oscar – and his dad just showed up and caused a big fuss about it all.'

'Oh,' Angus said, raising an eyebrow. 'Well that makes everything *much* clearer.'

Maggie gave him a look. 'It's complicated.' She shook her head. 'Oscar's ill. He's dying.'

'Ach, I'm sorry, that's tough for someone so young, and it seems you're fond of him?' Angus said, eyes briefly passing over his brother's old chair.

'I guess,' Maggie admitted. 'He's…I just feel a connection there, I can't really explain it.'

Angus pointed to the letter again. 'This still doesn't explain why his dad is sending you a letter?'

'I don't know,' she said, staring at the black wax seal. 'He was pretty weird and rude to me yesterday. Maybe I shouldn't even read this.'

'Maybe.'

But Maggie couldn't bring herself to just ignore it – the Logan family were the only ones she'd ever come across that saw the world the way she did. A world full of ghosts. What if this letter had some answers? 'Do you mind if I take a moment…I know I've just started tonight, but-'

'No need to explain. Take as long as you need. Not like it's busy right now, only ghosts out tonight apparently,' he said with a chuckle, and Maggie found herself glancing to the bar where his brother's shadow sat.

She forced a smile, held the letter up and headed into the back room. She sat on one of the old bar stools and peeled open the letter, hands shaking. It was written in scrawling red ink, and there was an address at the top: *Tair House*. She took a deep breath and read.

Dear Margaret,

First, please allow me to apologise for my behaviour yesterday. Truth be told, I've been very worried about Oscar. He's not taking his limitations seriously, and his mother and I have been concerned for his wellbeing for a long time. He should be staying at home, not galivanting in bars, walking around the city in the rain after dark, and putting his health at risk. Things have obviously become tense between us, and I apologise for letting it spill out during our encounter. It is only because we love Oscar very much, because he means everything to us, that we were concerned about his whereabouts.

All this to say, it was however, a happy – perhaps fateful – coincidence that my son eventually stumbled into your bar. I knew I recognised something of you when I saw you, and then Oscar admitted why you two had met up in the first place. He told me that you're like us – that you can see the spirits in the city, the ghosts in the rain.

That is why I'm writing. I know why you are the way you are. It is a gift, not a curse, no matter what you might think of it.

Margaret, my dear, I've been looking for you for a long time. You see, I knew your mother. In fact – and I know after everything that this may come as a surprise, or may seem confusing – but she and I were married. I was, for a short time, your stepfather. It was such a tragedy what happened to her in the accident, and I believe that your grandmother, unfairly, blamed me for it. Blamed the house that your mother had grown up in. That you should have grown up in. But she stole you away from me. We could have still been a family, Maggie.

In time, I was remarried, and with Lucia, had Oscar. Sadly, he has always been afflicted by an illness, and that is in part why

I have always been overprotective. I understand that it is his life, and he thinks he knows best, but he has not been making good decisions lately. Though, I have to say, getting to know you was maybe the best decision he's made in a long time, and I am only sorry about how our first encounter after so long apart went.

My wife and I would love it if you would come to the house so we could talk properly. It is the weekend soon, and maybe you'll have some time to visit once you've had an opportunity to think about all of this. I imagine this will all be confusing and strange, but our door is open to you. I assume you don't remember it here – you were so young when your grandmother stole you away. But Margaret, my dear Margaret, I think it's time you come home. Tair House belongs to you as much as us, after all.

I look forward to meeting you under better circumstances.

All my best,
Xavier Logan

Maggie could barely breathe as she read and reread the letter. None of it made any sense. Her mother. Her grandmother. And she'd had a stepfather, once. She'd had a home. Apparently, she still did. And her gran had taken her away, because of what happened to her mother? If all of this was true, why had her gran kept it all from her. She folded the letter back up and put it in the envelope. For a long time she sat in the chair and stared at the front of the envelope, where *Margaret Fall* had been written in such careful lettering. She thought back to the pictures she'd looked up the previous night, of Xavier Logan as a young man, a performer, and tried to think if she remembered anything of him from before. How had he met her mother? How had they ended up married? So many questions whirred in her mind. The dark room around her suddenly felt oppressive and dizzying, and she ran to the corner and threw up in the mop bucket. Not her finest moment. Even a rogue shadow moved away from her as if retreating from the smell.

She sat on the floor for a while, breathing and trying not to panic.

There was a knock on the door eventually, and Angus popped his head round it.

'Are you…' He spotted her by the bucket. 'Ah, oh dear, what's happened? You look like you've seen a ghost.'

Maggie looked up at him, wiped her face on her sleeves then she started to laugh.

His thick brow furrowed. 'Something I said?'

She shook her head. 'Kind of. Not really. I don't know… my head's all muddled.'

'This about that letter?' he asked. 'Knew that old guy was bad news as soon as he walked in. Should have sent him packing.'

Maggie pondered what to tell him. He was the only one in her life she could tell anything to, apart from Arlo and Gran's ghost. Maybe the truth was best. Or at least part of the truth. She'd leave the bit about the ghosts out – she still wanted to keep her job, it was the only thing she had left that wasn't completely falling apart. 'Apparently, he's my stepfather. Or was, for a very short time. Back…back before my mum died, they were married.'

Angus's frown deepened, and he glanced out the door to check the bar before walking in and sitting on one of the spare stools. 'And that other lad, Jack, or Oscar, was it?'

'Oscar.'

'He's your what?'

She shrugged. 'I mean, he's Xavier's son, but he must have been born after all that happened.'

Angus looked thoughtful, his eyes glimmering slightly in the pale light of the storeroom. 'Fancy a drink, I can close up early?'

'We've only just opened.'

'All good, too much rain tonight anyway, I'll pop a notice on the door, claim water damage or something. Really not a problem, this is more important.'

Her body untensed and she pushed the mop bucket to the side. 'Thanks Angus.'

'Maybe some food too, I'll see what I can rustle up,' he said. 'Just come out when you're ready and cleaned up.'

*

When Maggie came back out into the bar, Angus had set up a table with a couple of whisky drams with ice, and an array of crisps, cashews, and mini shortbread.

She sat and took some of the food to settle her stomach. Angus waited for her to speak before saying anything, and for a while they just sat in silence, occasionally taking sips, picking at the food.

'I should go there,' she said eventually. 'I should hear what he has to say.'

Angus nodded slowly. 'If you don't, would you always be curious?'

'Yeah,' she said. 'I guess so.'

'You know,' Angus began quietly, 'My brother and I weren't related, not by blood anyway.'

'Really?'

'Yeah,' he said. 'I was adopted when I was about two, but everyone always thought we were twins we looked so alike. Sometimes you're born into family, sometimes it finds you.'

'That's a nice thing.' Maggie smiled up at him. 'So, were you ever curious about your biological family?'

'Aye, I'd be lying if I said no, but then I thought, I'm sure they had their reasons,' he said. 'But if this is someone who wants to get to know you, maybe you can still hear him out.'

'I just keep wondering why my gran kept it all from me,' she said. 'What was so bad that she didn't want me to know it all?'

Angus nodded. 'Hmm. Your gran really told you nothing about him? About the house?'

She shook her head. What else had her gran kept from her? 'I could have had this whole other family, this other life, and instead it was just the two of us scraping by on what we had.'

'And here you were, rich all this time, owning some big manor house, and you've been working in this dead-end bar with me, eh,' he said, with a smile.

'I like working here,' she said. 'And I don't know what he wants. He could be lying about it all.'

Angus waved a hand, his cheeks slightly rosy. 'You don't owe him your time if you don't want to go. You can pretend you never got the letter, move on. You've managed all this time, shouldn't be too hard. And maybe that'd be for the best. Less complications.'

Maggie thought about it and stared at the flickering candlelight in the table. 'Though, I think he might know things,' she said carefully, working through her feelings about all of it. 'About who I am, about what I…about who my mother was, and I want to know.'

'Well then,' he said. 'That's settled, when will you go?'

Maggie turned the letter over, looking for a phone number or anything to arrange the visit. But all that was listed was the address. 'Do you think I could…I mean, he said I should come at the weekend, so I could think about it, but what if I talk myself out of it? So maybe I could have the night off tomorrow and go then? Just get it over and done with, so I can figure out the rest.'

'Course, whatever you need, as long as you come back,' he said. 'Can't lose my best bartender because she's suddenly discovered she's heir to some fancy fortune.'

'Of course I'll come back, if there's a job still waiting for me. I promise, Angus. You're like family, you know.'

'As are you Maggie,' he said with a warm smile.

She hesitated for a moment, pondering her conversation with Oscar in the bar days before. 'Angus,' she said to him carefully. 'How long has the bar been opened here now?'

He frowned, rolling his shoulders back. 'Ach, I don't know, I hardly keep count these days.'

'But you've always been in the city, you've never left?'

He shook his head, and his eyes drifted to fix on something over her shoulder. 'I suppose that's true,' he said slowly. 'Where else would I go?'

'Yeah, I suppose.'

She could see his attention drifting, his head tilted slightly to the side. His jaw was moving, like he was speaking, but no words were coming out.

A little unnerved, she stood up and started to clean up , putting away their glasses and makeshift dinner. The whole time, Angus remained sat there, so still, with his eyes fixed on that same spot. When it came time for closing, she had to wave a hand in front of his face just to get his attention.

He blinked rapily, then smiled up at her. 'Ah, is that you off, then?'

'Yeah, it's getting quite late,.'

He stood up so quickly he nearly knocked the table over, but he didn't react. He only pointed to the door. 'Don't forget your umbrella now,' he said. 'The rain is heavy tonight.'

The House

Inside Tair House, there is a kind of cold that seeps into everything. It is a place where ghosts don't keep their distance when they choose to come out, and where the living must give way to the dead.

The place is a mishmash of rooms, with winding staircases leading between levels, and dark corners everywhere. There are places the house keeps hidden, though, until the secrets they hold are ready to be revealed. The house often hears these secrets, spoken in the dead of night, and keeps them held safely in its walls. Whispers from below, and from beyond, stretching into its foundations until it is unsure whether the secrets are its secrets to hold, or if they belong to the other residents. Sometimes, the house thinks it can remember walking outside its grounds, though that was long ago, and it knows that this isn't something houses ordinarily do. It must be confused, it thinks, and when it experiences such moments, it hushes the thoughts and returns into itself, to watch from a distance for a time, while the grey world outside solidifies, and the clouds in the distant city of endless rain thunder louder, until the city itself may soon drown in water and spirits from the torrent that breaks free. For lately, the bind on the spirits is weakening. The ghosts grow stronger, more solid. More intent on being seen. That was, until the man of the house returned, and wrote a letter. To a woman with a name the house recognises. A name that started Tair House's entire ordeal. The Fall family. The house knows the family well. Theirs is a name built into its very foundations, ever since the day it first woke. The house knows, and the spirits know, and soon enough, the woman will know too. When she does, she will surely come to understand what it is she must do. And if she doesn't, there are ways to make her. Too long the house has been wandering and waning. This woman with her ghosts is the one it's been waiting for.

Tair House

Maggie left for Tair House early the next morning after feeding Arlo. Just as she'd left, she'd popped in to visit her gran, and had taken a photo out of the frame, the one of her with her mum on the stairs. In Tair House, she knew now. She turned it over, half expecting to see a scrawl at the bottom. Something she'd missed before that would explain the house, their presence there, and the man who called himself her former stepfather. But of course, there were no words on the pictures, just worn edges and marks of wear and tear. She still flattened it out and put it inside a notebook in her bag. Then she turned to Gran and stared at the chair.

'Why didn't you tell me?' she asked the shadowy figure. 'Why did you take me away from there?'

The only response was the slight tilt of the chair, her Gran barely an outline in the darkened room rocking slightly back and forth as if in rhythm to a slow humming music. She left the door to the room open – Arlo liked to sit in there and watch Gran – and headed out.

It was still raining, but not as torrentially as the day before. There were puddles in potholes though, and she spotted a couple of ghosts standing in them, half of their body more solid than the rest. She couldn't shake the feeling they were watching her. That as she walked past them, their heads would turn and they would follow her all along the way to the house. Though, in reality their only movement was a slow swaying as they whispered or mumbled in hushed disjointed tones.

She followed the directions on her phone, taking it out occasionally to get her bearings, her umbrella held firm in her other hand. She walked past Rose Way and took a shortcut up from Wallace's Smile towards the posh part of the city. Here, houses were old but perfectly preened. There were fancy cars outside, though weeds grew around the edges of them like they were rarely used. These were the type of houses where the rooms always looked uninhabited, everything organised, no clutter, but that loved to place the most prominent or expensive item easily on display – like a grand piano in their huge sitting rooms, or an indistinct painting that took up half the wall and shouted of its expense with its gold gilded frame. Some of them had ghosts standing in the garden, others with shadows just visible in brighter corners. She hurried past them and the next turn led her along winding quiet streets lined with tall oak trees and thick hedges that hid the buildings on the other side. An even grander kind of wealth, the kind that didn't like to be seen. Her gran used to tell her to never trust such places, and would rarely come to this side of town if she could help it.

Finally, as the houses grew sparser, more spaced apart from one another, she began a slight downward decline. In the distance, at the bottom of a hill, was a cemetery. The air turned cold as she descended. She lifted her shoulders up to her ears as her breath formed a fog with every step. The cemetery was at the bottom of the dip, and she entered through large cast-iron gates which were bleeding rust from the constant rain.

The rain as she traversed the rows of moss-covered headstones, and black stone crypts, became lighter to a small drizzle. Maggie had always liked spending time in cemeteries, and this city had many of them. For her, they were quiet places to sit and reflect, and she would go there because of the absence of the dead. Most of Maggie's ghosts tended to haunt the places they'd died, or their favourite places where they'd lived, like her gran in her chair, and the Green Man with his hedge. Cemeteries weren't common places for either conditions, so they were one of the only places in this city she could come and be confident not to be disturbed by anything other than a rook or magpie or two.

She followed the path between the gravestones to the other side of the cemetery, out a small gap half obscured by rhododendron so it could be easily missed, leading to a private side road. There at the end of the road, an old set of iron gates loomed, cleaner than the first. On either side of it ran tall stone walls, with creeping ivy and an overgrown garden beyond. The gate hung open towards a gravelstone road, where in the shade of a towering grey tree, almost concealed by thick undergrowth and a low mist, was the outline of a house. Above the gate, a wrought iron archway had been twisted into the lettering: *Tair House*.

Maggie steeled herself and entered through the second gate. Then, something very strange happened. As she stepped over the threshold to the other side, there was a sudden quiet. No sound of rain pitter-pattering on her umbrella. She closed it and looked up. The clouds above were dark and billowing, obscuring the sky so that it looked almost like she'd been plummeted into dusk. But it wasn't raining. She thought back, trying to remember a time she'd last been outside when it wasn't raining. But she couldn't. Even her umbrella was worn, the varnish on the wooden handle slightly faded where her fingers gripped it. She would venture to the seaside, and the rain would follow with a thick haar from the sea. She would wander up the seven hills of the city, and still she would sit amongst the clouds, and the rain would pour, and the cold and wet would bleed into her skin, and the ghosts would gather in amongst it. Here, it was dry. No figures standing near, no ghosts to haunt her step – not the visible kind, at least. The ground around the path was an array of cracked soil and dead grass, only the hardiest of plants remaining: rhododendron, bracken, thorny bushes of brambles and blackberries. Two jackdaws flew above her and landed on a withered tree to her left, rested on its black branches and chittered away above. She clipped the umbrella to her bag and carried on into the cold, footsteps crunching eerily in the bone-dry stillness.

The house soon loomed into view, a grand façade of mismatched stones and sash windows built over three floors. Maggie paused to properly take it all in, trying to understand how she could have forgotten living here. It wasn't exactly the kind of house to readily forget. Though, it wasn't currently seeing its best years, and was in desperate need of repairs – a broken chimney of crumbling stone, thin fractures running along the sides of the walls, a towered spire leaning sideways, and missing roof tiles leaving a patchwork of slate and exposed wooden beams. Beyond the house the rest of the city was obscured by a forest of grey trees, barely a leaf surviving amongst them.

At the front of the house stood a single ash tree that looked half-burnt, its trunk bent inwards towards the house, as if it had sunk sideways into the ground. Its form groaned despite the absence of wind, branches reaching out like they were trying to touch the house itself. Below it, the only thing that had survived with greenery to spare were more bramble bushes, the fruit overripe or rotten, and bleeding crimson juices into the frosty ground, staining it red.

'*Don't go back. never go back.*' Maggie froze still, staring at the house, her mum's words from her dreams feeling suddenly clear and sharp. Was it a memory? There was an urgency in the voice as she heard them repeated in her mind, an out of breath rasp in the rush of them. Had her mum meant this house? Maybe she shouldn't have come here after all.

Though, how could she come all this way and just leave, when she was so close to remembering, to knowing what had happened in her past that had made her forget? And, there was something about this cold and dark nook of the city that made her feel like she might finally see through the rain and fog that had haunted her for so long. She shivered again and moved towards the front of the house up the driveway. There was a silver car outside with its windows blacked out, the only polished thing in the grounds. She looked up at the house, took in its immense size. There were a couple of dim lights in the windows, but most were covered in a black dust or frost, shuttered or with curtains drawn to keep the light or cold out. The doorway was a grand arch, the columns on either side carved with intricate stone patterns of ivy and thorns. The stairway that led to the main door was covered in clumps of shrivelled weeds, as if they'd burst free from between the grout and died at the sight of the house looming above them.

The door itself was painted with dark red paint, peeling and revealing woodworm-infested panels underneath. Maggie approached it hesitantly, put her hand on the cold stone column and tried to remember if she'd ever stood here, on this very threshold, before. The door knocker was a large brass moth, and just as she reached forward to knock it, the door opened wide.

A tall greying man with a charcoal peacoat smiled down at her.

'Oh! Margaret, my dear,' Xavier said, and she flinched slightly at the term, and the enthusiasm in his voice – a stark change from the coffee shop. 'So, you got my letter? You're earlier than I expected, but not to worry.' He held out his hands in welcome, as if he planned to lean out and hug her. She didn't return the gesture, so after a few seconds of standing in awkward silence, he dropped his arms, moved to the side, and ushered her through.

Tentatively she stepped inside the house.

The first thing she noticed was the dryness of the air. It caught in her throat, along with the scent and woodsmoke, though there was no warmth. The ceilings were tall, making the space draughty, and she looked up to see wallpaper and paint peeling and the corners of the ornate white cornicing cracking. She lowered her gaze to the space instead, a grand hallway with a dark wooden staircase beyond. In the entranceway itself was an array of unkempt dark wooden furniture, a chest of drawers with handles missing, side tables crooked with uneven legs, moth-holed curtains, and worn carpets with threads sticking out from the edges. Everything was covered in what looked like multiple layers of dust and ash. There was a fire lit beside the stairs, but it burned feebly in the corner next to a sad pile of already blackened wood, giving off no heat. Maggie wrapped her arms around herself and turned to Xavier, not making eye contact. 'So…I lived here once?'

Xavier nodded. 'Yes, it maybe looked a little different back then. Old houses are hard to maintain, and expensive mind. But come. I'll make us some tea, unless you'd prefer whisky?' There was a glimmer in his eyes.

Maggie raised an eyebrow. 'It's only mid-morning.'

He looked out the closest window, squinting as if the light was too bright for him. 'Hmm. Yes of course, so it is. So hard to tell with everything so grey, isn't it?'

Maggie followed him up a set of three small steps to the living room, noticing a broken cuckoo clock sitting in an alcove as she went, with the bird hanging crooked from the little box, one wing missing. Both clock hands had stopped below the twelve.

The drawing room was vast and cold, with ceilings so high that the light from the half-shuttered windows didn't reach the top. Old chandeliers hung down from the centre. Maggie wondered if the electricity was broken – the only source of light other than the window were occasional candles occupying corner tables or dressers, and most of the lamps sat dusty and without bulbs. In the centre, was a plush seating area, dark green velvet sofas with grand wingback chairs either side with wooden details around the edges, facing a fireplace with half-charred wood within. The charred look even tracked up from it to the walls above, with speckles of soot underneath torn and cracking wallpaper. In the back of the room, was a grand piano, though a number of the keys were missing. A vague memory played in her mind of her sitting on her mum's lap as they played the piano together, slowly tapping at the keys. And her mum sang in a soft voice, an echoing lullaby, *'rain rain, go away'*. As she looked at the instrument, she could almost hear her mum's voice again, echoing in the space. On passing, she pushed one of the keys down, but the sound was dampened and out of tune. In the candlelight beyond the piano, a shadow moved across the wall and disappeared into a darkened corner.

'Every house has its ghosts,' Xavier said, noticing Maggie watching. 'Sorry about the piano, none of us play so we've not kept it working. That was always your mother's thing. Do you still play?'

Maggie shook her head. 'I'd forgotten I ever did.'

Xavier gave a sympathetic smile. 'It's the city,' he said. 'It likes us to hold memories at a distance.'

Maggie frowned. 'And this house?'

'I suppose it's special, in its way,' he said. 'Even the walls remember their past.'

She paused, trying to make sense of the cryptic way Xavier spoke, as if the place itself was alive.

'Shall we?' he spoke again, then guided her towards the back of the room. There, under another archway, were mirrored doors and Maggie jumped at the many reflections of herself. Some of the glass was cobwebbed with splintered fissures cutting her face in two. Xavier slid the doors open, leading to a separate enclosed dining room, curved with large windows and alcove seating around the entire wall, corners separated by tall bookcases. Most windows had been shuttered except for the one that faced outwards to the view of the old ash tree. White lichen stretched across one side of the trunk, sticking out from the crevices like tiny pale fingers, while the rest was dappled in charcoal-black burn marks.

'What happened to it?' she asked.

'One of the victims of the fire,' he said, a sadness in his voice.

'There was a fire?'

'Yes. Long before you were born. Before I even lived here,' he said. 'But the house lived on, at least.' He added, and ushered Maggie to the table where some delicate teacups had been laid out. 'Please, sit I won't be long, I'll put the kettle on. And I'll let Lucia know you're here, I expect she'll want to meet you too.'

Lucia? Oscar's mother, presumably. She wondered if Oscar would be joining them. There'd been no sign of him yet.

Xavier left her alone to ponder it all. To distract herself from the spinning thoughts, she wandered along the edges of the room. She tried to open one of the shutters, but they had been sealed over with paint. She moved on to test a few of the light switches on the wall. None worked. On the shelves there was an array of photo frames – empty, with all the photos removed. Soot lingered on the backing of a few, pressed up against the glass. There were some books too, old ones bound with leather or cloth. Most were covered in dust, except for a few on a middle shelf that looked more recently used. She peered at the spines, but none had titles – just symbols etched, in variations of triangles and sharp lines. A triangle with a cross through it, two triangles intersecting, another triangle upside down with a smaller one in its centre. She was sure she'd seen a shape like that before. Maggie reached to pull it from the shelf as the door slid open behind her.

'Don't touch those, please,' Xavier said. 'Antiques, you see, must be handled carefully.'

Maggie pulled her hand back but kept looking at the symbols. 'You collect them?'

He nodded. 'They're very important to me.'

'Were they to do with your…' she searched for the right word. 'Performances?'

'Ah, yes,' he said. 'You read about me I expect?'

'Yes, you and the Fearless Ferrante, was it? Do you still work with her?'

His smile tightened. 'My methodology has changed somewhat over the years. Used to be more thoroughfare about it all, but now I don't partake in public shows or tricks of fancy. The novelty, I suppose, wore off, and frankly most people didn't appreciate my practice.'

'So that's what they were, your shows. Just tricks?'

'In a manner of speaking,' he said. 'But that doesn't mean they weren't real.'

'I've read about mediums and spiritualists,' she said. 'Taking people's money, taking advantage of fear and grief.'

Xavier frowned and placed the teapot down on the table next to the teacups. 'Well, suppose these people get something from the experience? Closure, acceptance. Who are we to deny them that?'

'Hmm.'

'I'm surprised you're a sceptic, with your gift.'

'It's not a gift.'

'Ah,' he said. 'Well, I'm sorry you've grown up without the understanding of it, without someone to help you with it all. I could have helped you Maggie, if only you're grandmother had not acted so rashly.'

'Is that why you brought me here? Want me to join some spiritualist movement with you? For me to be your next *fearless* assistant.'

Xavier started laughing. 'Oh, no, no, nothing like that.' Then his expression changed, his sudden stare intent and unsettling. 'You really look like her, you know. Your mother.'

Maggie turned away from him towards the window, and she heard his slow breath as he picked up the teapot and poured it into the cups. A fragrant smell filled the room, herbal and floral.

'Please, sit,' he said. 'We don't have to talk about her straight away.'

Maggie rolled her shoulders back and sat, pulling the cup towards her, the heat of it welcome in her palms. Xavier offered her sugar but she declined. She took a small sip – it was bitter, so she added a cube of sugar after all. Across the table, Xavier was stirring his own cup slowly so that the spoon rattled in a disjointed rhythm against the cup.

'Why did you bring me here, then?' she asked after a pause.

'Why did you come?'

Maggie hesitated. 'I guess I wanted to know more about the ghosts, and what happened here, before when we lived here, and about my...' She trailed off as she found herself wondering whether her mum had died in this house. Had it been in this room? What if all that Xavier had to say about her mum were things she didn't want to hear?

Xavier leaned forwards and put his hands on the table, one of his fingers beginning to tap on the table, his long fingernail hitting the wood like the ticking of a clock. 'I know this is complicated, but I'll try and answer any questions you have, Maggie. So, please, ask away.'

Maggie didn't know where to start. 'Where's Oscar?' she asked first, wondering again why he wasn't here. Surely, he'd want to see her too. To understand how they were all connected. And part of her wanted a familiar presence in the room, to keep her company as her image of her past and world started to fall apart.

He clearly hadn't expected that line of questioning, but he leaned back a little, his eyes lifting to the ceiling above him. 'Oscar is sick.'

'Can I see him?' she said. 'I'd like to speak to him too… about all of this.'

'He's sleeping just now,' Xavier said. 'As I said, he's quite unwell, no doubt due to his…many recent forays into the city.' There was a hint of accusation in his voice, and a twinge of guilt crept into her stomach. It's not like she knew he was sick, he'd not exactly been forthcoming about it.

'I didn't know about that.'

'I understand, I don't blame you, my dear, not at all.' His eyebrows sharpened. 'Perhaps later once we've had a chance to catch up, then we can go up and see him, how does that sound?'

Maggie took another sip then sat back, her hands clenching on her legs. Behind Xavier, another shadow moved along the shutters and lingered a while on the wall beside the ash tree. For a moment, there was the blurred shape of a head, and it tilted slightly as if looking directly at her.

'Why don't I start by telling you about how your mother and I met?' Xavier broke the silence and Maggie's attention jumped away from the ghost back to him. He reached his hand across the table, as if to comfort her, and she felt a shiver move up her spine. She leaned back further. She shouldn't have come here. The quiet in the absence of the rain against the window was unnerving, too. When had she started to find comfort in the rain? It was, she supposed, the main constant thing in her life, until now.

'You said your wife, Lucia, was joining us?' she said feeling suddenly exposed, alone in this place. The shadow of the ghost in the gap was still watching her. Its hand had raised up now.

A gentle knocking was coming from somewhere in the house, like a branch hitting against a window.

'She will, she's just seeing to Oscar upstairs.' Xavier's turned to look where Maggie's eyes were fixed on the wall, and the ghost skulked away. 'We weren't expecting you to come so quickly,' he added. 'That maybe you'd need a day or two to think about it.'

'Then why didn't you leave a phone number, so I could call and arrange it?'

Xavier chuckled. 'Oh we don't get signal here,' he said. 'No electricity either. Old house,' he added as if that was enough of an explanation. 'In fact, we're very cut off from the city. I expect you noticed that.'

Maggie took her phone out and glanced at it. There was no signal and her feeling of unease crept up her throat. 'Maybe I should go, come back at the weekend then?'

'Not at all,' Xavier said, leaning forward. 'We'll be ready to get started soon.'

'What do you mean?'

He paused and looked at her for a long second. 'I only mean, why don't we get started? I can tell you all you want to know about your gift, about your mother. Isn't that why you came here?' He glanced to the doors behind her. His form in the reflection was a splintered array of jagged greys and blacks.

Maggie's heartrate was rising, but she hadn't found out what she needed to yet. 'Yes,' Maggie said. 'Okay. Can you tell me how she died?'

Xavier blinked once. 'That's what you want to know first?'

'My gran never told me exactly. She only said it was all a tragic accident. Was it here, in the house?' she asked. Maybe she was the woman Maggie had seen in the shadows.

'Yes,' Xavier said simply.

'And?'

Xavier sighed. 'There is context. It may not serve you best to tell you the cause, without telling you about the circumstances.'

Maggie stood up and the room spun a little. She felt dizzy, like the pieces in the mirror. 'I think I should go,' she said, but Xavier slammed a hand on the table.

'We were married on a Thursday,' he said suddenly, and Maggie froze in place. 'Your mother and I. It was a brisk autumn, one of those days where the skies were clear and blue. You wore a white dress with an autumn wreath in your hair. Your mother said you were the star of the day, not her. She was selfless like that. Do you remember it?'

Maggie didn't, though as he said the words there was something there – a little shard of something real. *Confetti on the ground. Bubbles dancing in the sky, reflecting the gleam of the low autumn sun. The smell of cinnamon and hot chocolate, and fiddle music, a ceilidh, dancing. The tap-tap of feet on wooden floors.* Above her, another tap-tap-tap, like a branch against the floor. Were these real memories, or conjured up by Xavier's words? 'Why are you telling me that?'

'It's relevant for the chain of events,' he said. 'It's important we don't miss out these details, how else can you understand it all.'

Maggie rubbed her arm and sat back down. 'Okay, so how did you meet?'

'Fate brought us together,' he said. 'And tragedy, I suppose. Such is the way of things, a balance of destinies, a light in the darkness.'

The man had a skill for speaking in riddles. When she

didn't say anything, Xavier smiled slightly and continued. 'We met at a party I was performing at.'

'My mother came to one of your shows?'

'Indeed. Such a lovely meeting it was. She stayed for the performance, and I'd be lying if I said I didn't notice her in the circle. She was striking, your mother. Though she had this sad, lost look about her. For someone so young, she had felt so much pain and loss. I could tell that right away. Your father, her parents, gone. You were the only blood relative she had left. She worried about you so much and wanted to keep you safe. In fact, she asked me to help.'

'You were older than her?' Maggie said, though from how he dressed, how grey his skin was, she found it hard to place his age. In some lights, she could think him closer to her gran's age.

'Age is but a number. We shared a similar spirit, and I knew what it was to lose someone. It was a deep connection, right from the start.'

Maggie resisted the urge to grimace. 'She was vulnerable.'

'We both were,' he said. 'Anyway, our relationship started off as one of business. She sought my help. And before you cast judgement, I did not agree lightly. To meddle with the spirit world, the veil, the other side, is dangerous work. Though she was eager to start, I knew we'd have to wait for the right time when the veil was thin enough.'

'And then?'

'Then we fell in love,' he said as if it were as inevitable as the rain. 'With time, we realised we had much in common. Both of us were widowers, I had lost my love too young, and she—'

'Fearless Ferrante?' Maggie interjected.

Xavier's shoulders tensed. 'Yes.'

'How did *she* die?'

'That's not what we're here to talk about, is it?'

'I just wondered if you have a habit of people dying around you?'

'Considering your own family's past, I'd expect that you know the feeling,' Xavier said with a terse look. 'Now, did you want to hear the rest of the story, or not?'

Maggie took a deep breath, feeling increasingly like Xavier was not the charming front of a man he had been putting up since she'd arrived here. 'Fine. So you were married, then what?'

'Well, our fates, as it were, became entwined. We were wed. We lived here, the three of us. Happily for a time. It is a sadness you don't remember that, my dear.'

'Did you do the spirit…communicating, ritual, whatever it is she'd wanted you to do?'

'No, in time, she realised it wouldn't help her get closure. And with me there, she felt safe, felt that you were too, and you were the one she was most worried about. Most protective of. She didn't want you to be taken by the same curse she believed her family to have been.'

'But she did die, she was taken.'

'Yes.' A dark look fell across his face. 'A tragic accident. She fell carrying you. Down the basement. You were so littleat the time it is no wonder you do not remember. Tragedy is easy to forget in the mind, even if it sticks with you somewhere deep inside, etched into your very being.' He paused for a second, rubbing his eye as if to brush away tears, though his eyes were as dry as the air around them. 'She positioned her body to protect you from the fall, so you were only injured slightly.'

Surely she would have remembered something like that.

'It was how I realised it was you, in the coffee shop, I saw that distinctive scar of yours.' He grabbed her wrist and traced his thumb along the edges of the cut. His hand was so cold, but his grip was strong.

Maggie's head began to spin, images swirling in her mind. *Blood, candlelight, a deep voice, words she didn't understand.*

'Your mother died in my arms, with you by her side,' Xavier said in a quiet voice.

Darkness and rotting roots stretching out from stone. Her mother reaching out, asking for help.

He finally let her go, and Maggie shook the image away. 'There were...it was dark.'

'Dark? I suppose it was,' he said, leaning back now, watching her carefully. 'Does this mean you remember it?'

'No...I...I don't know. It's all a haze. But there were others there, another voice, after she....' Maggie clutched her head. What was happening?

Xavier leaned forwards again, his fists clenched tight on the table by the teapot. Maggie noticed his teacup was still full, where hers lay empty in front of her.

'You saw the ghosts, perhaps?' he suggested.

'No, there was another woman there,' she said, the confusing tangle of images arranging and rearranging in her mind. Were they memories? Then she could see a face clearly, a woman dressed all in black. 'She was wearing a funeral shroud, black netting over her face,' she spoke it out loud as she remembered it.

'Maybe you are thinking of your grandmother,' Xavier said. 'She arrived at the house for a visit and found us. After her son died, she often dressed in black.'

'No that's...it's not her.'

'She blamed me, blamed the house and she took you up in her arms and swept you away. If I'd known you were so close all this time...I did look for you, Maggie. Your grandmother moved from her old address, and I found no record of you at all. It was like you'd disappeared into the rainy city, never to be seen again. Until I saw you in the café.'

Maggie stood up, though she didn't feel like herself. The room was spinning. Something was wrong. Was it only the memories returning making her feel so out of place, as if her body was folding in on itself. She made to leave, to get some fresh air, but Xavier walked to the door and blocked her way out. 'You look ill? Should I get you some-'

'No,' she pushed him away. 'I need to get out of here. I need to go home.'

'Maybe you just need a lie down,' he said, speaking fast. 'I understand this is probably a lot to take in, remembering, things you've not thought about in so long. Must be quite disorienting.'

'No, just...get out of my way,' she said shaking him away. 'I'm leaving.'

Xavier stared at her, and Maggie thought he was about to grab her again like the Green Man had, like Oscar on his first night in the bar had taken her arm, told her she looked familiar. Now that she thought about it, why had he thought she looked familiar? Had he seen pictures of her? Or pictures of her mother, if they looked so alike? She wished Oscar was here now, that he could help her make sense of it all. That she wasn't alone here with his father and a room full of ghosts and broken things.

Just as Maggie was considering shoving the old man into the wall, Xavier stepped aside with a sigh, and slid the doors open. She stumbled out into the drawing room and tried to catch her hitching breaths. The room kept spinning as she walked. Shadows moved across the walls, flickering in the dim candlelight. There was a thump from upstairs, a louder bang than she'd heard earlier. What was up there? She looked up at the ceiling, unable to see through the dark to the top. A chandelier creaked back and forth with a non-existent wind. When she dropped her gaze back to the room itself, a woman was standing there. A woman with a black dress and a funeral shroud. A coldness swept across the room, and Maggie's vision blurred. She took a step back and fell. Arms caught her before she hit the ground – Xavier, his grip firm on her shoulders. Then, the woman was standing over her, her form a strange distortion – like she was half a ghost caught in the rain. All grey and black except for her crimson-red gloves. Then her voice came, rasping and disjointed.

'I'm sorry I didn't come sooner,' the shrouded woman said.

'It matters not. We had much to talk about. I kept her busy.'

Busy?

'Good.'

'Is everything ready my fearless love?'

'Soon. I need some time to prepare. As does the house,' the woman said, and above her, a large black moth fluttered rising up into the dark ceiling above. 'Tomorrow we will begin.'

'The tea will keep her rested until then,' Xavier said, and Maggie felt her body go weak, even though she wanted to fight it, to run from this house and never come back. She was a dead weight. Where was Oscar? She tried to cry out for him, but no words came out.

Behind the woman the shadows had gathered in the doorway above, some of them reaching out into the dark. Maggie tried to grab them, calling upon her ghosts to help her, just this once. But her hands only found thin dry air.

The House

Long ago a woman and her daughter lived in this house. Their lives were connected to the house even if they did not understand it. But the house remembers. It remembers what their family did, long before. What their family took from the house, what they should have given it in return. The house is bitter – it feels it in its foundations, its dark and hidden crevices, and in the roots of the ash tree that have broken through its walls. Bitterness is like that – it seeps in, and it infects all that surrounds it.

When the man stepped foot in the house again, the house rejoiced. He had been here before – the house recognised him even though the years had aged him, leaving him grey and wrinkled, with deep sunken eyes, and a hard cold stare. He had been the reason the house had awoken in the first place, years before, and the house had missed him. The house had been stuck in limbo for too long, its reach limited to its darkening grounds. Now, the house was hopeful. The house remembered what it wanted.

The house was hungry.

The house was ready to become alive again, and the young girl of the house was the key. All great things come at a cost. Sacrifice is a necessary evil. And the house yearned for a revenge long sought, for a payment long demanded.

The house could taste the closeness of freedom with its mortar and stone, feel the gap between its forever slumber and almost-living shrink.

The man plotted and finally, the man struck.

The girl screamed. The girl cried. The girl bled.

The mother wailed.

The house was finally alive again, not just trapped in a distant slumber. For the first time in many years, it was truly waking up.

But there is always a catch. The new man of the house had been foolish. He underestimated a mother's love. A lock on the door was not enough to hold her there as he took her daughter. The mother opened the window, leapt out into the night, and with a limp, came to find her young daughter, before the house could fully take her for itself.

The house was not yet strong enough to stop her, though it tried. It failed, and the mother ran. The mother took what belonged to the house, the young girl, and took her away, out of reach, where neither the house nor the man of the house could find her.

The house felt itself waning, felt the gap between the two worlds weaken again. It did not want to go back to the way it was before.

But then, hope, for the mother came back. Foolish, too, but fortunate. She came for the man of the house, but he was the wrong target, for the house was now awake, and so too was a new woman of the house. A woman who had slept for too long, who had lived inside the house, out of sight, out of mind, remembered by none other than the house itself and the spirits within. And with the ritual finally complete after all this time and the binds between the dead and the living broken, the ghosts too began to break through, spilling out from the walls of the house, beyond the grounds and into the grey city of rain to find their new homes.

The house would have preferred to take the girl that night, but the mother was enough. Enough for a time to keep the house awake and living. To keep Tair House safe, the ghosts free, and the rain coming endlessly in the city adjacent.

The house was hungry, and so, the house would feed.

Dreams in the dark

A knife on Maggie's arm, pushing down, cutting into flesh. Two precise marks, one up, one down. An incomplete triangle, a ritual begun. White-hot pain then a darkness.

A song ringing out, words chanted in the night. A woman in the dark. A woman with hands that reach, and a shroud that conceals. Hands reaching for her. Closer, the woman is ready to become, to be summoned anew. The house holding its breath.

A break in the circle, in the ritual. Not again, not when everything is so close. A figure, this one alive, stepping in. Wrenching away.

Her mum carrying her in her arms. Running. Gravel crunching underfoot.

Her mum out of breath. Tears. Blood. Warm and cold all at once. Then another figure in the dark. This one familiar. Her gran. Hands reaching out to protect this time.

'I got your message, what happened?'

'Take her.' A voice, breathless. Desperate. 'Take her and never come back.'

'Evelyn. What happened?

'There's no time. She's not safe here, please, take her away.'

Her mum letting her go, pushing her into her gran's arms.

'What about you?' her gran's voice. 'Come with us.'

'I have to stop him. I have to make him see sense. I need to end this.'

'Evelyn, she needs her mother.'

'I'll come back. Just hide somewhere safe. Away from the house. Away from the city if you can.'

A shout in the distance. A man's voice, yelling, *'Evelyn. Bring her back! You don't understand what you will unleash!'*

'What are you going to do?' Gran's voice, shaking.

'We should have let the house burn long ago. And that's exactly what I'll do if I must, before he can do any more evil here.'

A kiss on her forehead. 'I love you, Maggie. I'll find you again.' Then, her mum gone, running back towards the house.

Maggie crying. A new spattering of rain on her cheeks as they leave the house. Black clouds rolling above and beyond. Her mum disappearing into the dark. Maggie in her gran's arms, running between rows of headstones. The first time she saw a ghost, a figure standing by the cemetery gates in the rain, reaching out a hand to her as she passed. And Maggie reaching out her hand, her arm thick with her own blood where the cut had been made. Looking back over her gran's shoulder at the looming house behind as dark clouds descend and the rain starts to fall in the city, never to stop.

*

The light was dim when Maggie awoke from a fitful sleep. She'd been dreaming of her mum again – clearer than normal, like a memory. A memory of the house, and her mum, and her gran, and a cut on her arm. She thumbed the scar, and an image of metal on her skin flashed through her mind once more. Not of a fall or accident, but a purposeful cut. She could feel the sting of it now as if it were just a moment ago. Shivering, she sat up.

The room around her was disorienting and shadows tapered across the cracked and crumbling walls. She was somewhere in the house still. The memory of the day before flooded back to her, of Xavier and the woman that was both a ghost and not a ghost standing above her. She sat up straight.

There was a sharp chill in the air, and there was a musky scent, lavender mixed with the tang of burning oil. The oil lamp that burned in the corner of the room was the only source of light. Its flame flickered, dancing dark and light across the walls. She looked towards it and noticed there were eyes staring at her from the chair in the corner of the room. A ghost, watching, more solid than it should be in the dry. But then this house wasn't like the city – maybe the ghosts had different rules here. She pulled the cover off slowly and slid out of bed. She was barefoot, her feet landing on the rough exposed woodworm-holed floor. Cold. For a moment there was the memory of Xavier's hands on her, of the woman in the shroud, as he carried her upstairs. She shivered as wind crept through the cracks in the shutters and walls, making the loose wallpaper flutter like gills. In the corner, a moth fluttered to the lamp and rested next to it, wings stretching and settling out, eyes angled towards her. She was only wearing a light white set of pyjamas, so she grabbed a moth-holed dressing gown that was hanging on the side of the wardrobe to the left of the bed to cover herself up.

Then, she tiptoed forwards towards the lamp and picked it up as the moth flew away into the dark above. She tried to ignore the ghost in the chair. But he was watching her. She was sure of it. This ghost was solid. Grey, like the others in the rain, but his face in the light as she moved closer to him wasn't as featureless as the others.

He shared her green-grey eyes, and the freckles that dappled cheeks. And though he was older, faded, as if pulled from an old-fashioned photograph, she recognised him from the look in his eyes. From the photos that still lived in her gran's room by her rocking chair.

Her dad. It took all she could not to cry out to him as she realised. He was unmoving, surveying her with an intense curiosity. There was no colour in his face, and he tilted his head slightly to one side, then to the other, like he was a slowly bobbing jack in the box. As he did his neck came adrift from his body, blurred into the background of the shadow.

'Maggie,' came a whisper. His lips cracked slightly as they opened. 'You shouldn't have come back. Leave this place, now. Run.'

'Dad? What happened here? What did Xavier do? What happened to Mum?'

'No good can come of this. I'm sorry Maggie,' he repeated. He lifted his hand pointing to the door. A caterpillar clung to his bony finger, head down as if chewing on his faded grey skin. Maggie fought back the urge to look away. 'You need to-' And then the oil lamp blinked out, leaving her in darkness. She fell back, dropping the lamp, which broke open. The oil drenched the dressing gown and her feet. The smell of it stuck in her throat, and her breath hitched. She waited for her dad to say anything more, for him to speak to her but no words came.

When she stumbled back and hit something solid, she yelped slightly. But it was just the bedpost. Her eyes adjusting to the dark, she could just make out the door to the hall outside. Leaving the broken lamp behind, and bringing with her the oil-slick smell, she tried the doorknob but it was locked. She felt around to try to find a key, but there was none. On the doorframe, there were scraping marks, splinters of wood as if someone had once tried to break the door open.

Feeling her way around the room, she found a candlestick on the panelled windowsill with half a candle left. In one of the bedside table drawers, she found a small box of matches. The tips were worn down, and it took a few tries to spark them, but eventually she got the candle lit. Holding it aloft, she looked around the space for a way out. Her dad's ghost was gone from the chair, though she felt still like someone was watching her. She raised the candle higher and found she wasn't wrong. Moths lined the ceiling above her, clustered together, hundreds of eyes glinting red in the candlelight. In the corners, their grey cocoons hung like hundreds of tiny stalactites.

Maggie shivered and looked away, searching the room instead for anything else that would help her make sense of what the hell was going on. She found herself tracking her hands across the flowery wallpaper, with green edges that were faded and torn. Something about the room felt so familiar. Because she'd been here before. It was her mother's room.

There was an antique bureau in the corner, and she went to it first, took down the folding table. Most of the shelving gaps were home to only dust, but there was a single photo frame face down inside, which she pulled out. In it was a picture of a baby held in the arms of her parents, standing outside Tair

House. Maggie tilted the candlestick towards it to look closer, saw the smiling face of her parents, blue skies and sunshine above. Part of the photo had been torn off in the centre, leaving the bottom left of the house missing. Maggie searched around in the small drawers beneath the desk. In one she found a fragment of paper in the next. The missing piece had just a window in it that looked as though someone had tried to scrape out the ink from the painting. But visible, just out the corner of the window was the outline of a woman wearing a shroud. Maggie stared at it. The woman from downstairs. Had this woman been here all this time? How did she end up tied to Xavier?

Maggie put the fragment down and opened the cupboard part at the base of the desk. Some of the handles creaked with disuse, while inside caterpillars wriggled along the walled edges. A layer of dust coated the shelves themselves, forgotten and untouched for a long time. Avoiding the insects at the edges, she carefully rifled through papers, photos, printouts about the house. She found a small bundle of sage next to a book about protection against curses in the modern world that was full of illustrations making it look like a fanciful reference book rather than for genuine use. Inside it was a piece of card. She slipped it out, reading the golden embossed words beyond. It was an invitation:

Dear Evelyn Fall of Tair House,

As a resident of one of the city's foremost houses, it is my pleasure to invite you to an exclusive evening of spiritualism and mediumship. I was sorry to hear of the passing of your parents, and most recently, your husband. You may not remember me, but we have met once before when you were younger. Your father was a fan of my abilities, and often attended my events.

I have since been travelling, and have learnt much on my journey and look forward to expanding my practice. Perhaps it could help offer some comfort in light of your recent losses. It would therefore be my pleasure to welcome you to one of my exclusive parties as an honorary guest.

I look forward to meeting you.

All my best,
Xavier Logan

Maggie felt a stirring in her gut. Was this the party her mother had met Xavier? He'd said it was by chance, but here it was clear he'd invited her. He'd mentioned her mother's family – her grandfather. What connection had they had? How had he known of Tair House before he'd even met her mother?

Around her, she could almost feel the house close in. Could almost hear her mother's voice, telling her to leave, to never come back. Why hadn't Maggie just listened to her doubts when she'd arrived. Pocketing the invite, she closed the cupboard and tried the door again. It rattled on the latch but wouldn't open. When she tried the shutters by the window, they'd been sealed shut like the ones downstairs, even as she pried with fingernails along the edges. One of her nails caught in the gap and half snapped off with the effort.

'She cursed, instinctively pulling her hand to her mouth. Her nailbed bled, and the taste of blood was metallic, tinged with a bitter taste of the oil from the lamp. She wrapped it in a piece of paper from the desk and took a deep breath. As the blood soaked through the paper, a moth descended from above and landed on her hand, edging towards the paper. Then another, and another, until nearly a dozen were encircling her wrist.

'Go away,' she shouted at it, shaking them off. They fluttered upwards together, seeming to merge for just a moment, before rising to the ceiling. They joined the others, hundreds of wings now fluttering in unison, creating a strange humming noise above. Almost like they were groaning. What the hell was with this place?

She thought now about how only Arlo and the ghost of her gran knew where she'd gone. Though she'd told Angus about the letter and Xavier's name, she'd not exactly given him the address. When she didn't show up at work, how long before he came to check up on her to find her gone? At least she'd left enough food for Arlo for a couple of days. After that… what if Xavier never let her leave? What did they even have planned for her? Maybe they planned to feed her to the moths, she thought, resisting the urge to look up at the ceiling. The memories of the dream and the woman in the shroud filled her mind again with a black and crimson haze as she tried to find an explanation for it.

She felt trapped. Could almost feel the walls closing in. Placing the candlestick to the side of the door, she knelt down and put an eye against the keyhole as she tried the doorknob again. There was a dim light coming from the hallway, from a candle or oil lamp. Then there was a sound at the other side. Footsteps. A shadow. Then an eye, looking straight at her. She fell back and crawled on her hands backwards. A key in the door. The doorknob twisted, and Maggie scrambled to find anything she could to protect herself. She picked up the modern curses book from the desk and held it at the ready.

Then the figure walked through the door, grey-skinned and surrounded by shadows.

A reunion

'Maggie?'

She looked out into the gloom and lowered the book. A dishevelled figure looked back at her. She could have cried out in relief. 'Oscar?' she hissed.

When he stepped forwards and closed the door lightly, Maggie stepped back again.

'What the hell is going on?' she asked.

'I was going to ask you the same thing.'

'It's your dad…he…I think he poisoned me or something, and your mum, is she…'

'The one with the black shroud?' he finished for her, his voice barely a whisper. 'Yes.'

'Is she a ghost?'

He frowned and shook his head. 'No. I don't know really, I mean, she had me, but she's always been…different. And lately she's been getting sicker. As if she's just becoming one of them again.'

Maggie noticed the way the dark circles had formed under Oscar's eyes, the greyness in his complexion, his lips dry and cracked, his fingernails black on his hands. 'Are you…' *Are you dead?* she wanted to ask, but how could he be? 'What are you?' she asked instead.

Oscar just blinked at her. 'What do you mean?'

'You look like her.'

'She's my mother.'

'No, you look like her. Your skin, your hands.'

'I told you, I'm dying.' Oscar stepped towards her and in the candlelight, Maggie saw the softness of his expression. The way there was light there, like she'd seen in the darkness of the bar. 'Though, honestly, I'm not sure I ever was living,' he admitted. 'But I was born, and I have grown up, aged, but now…Well, I'm fading like my mother.'

'I don't understand.'

'Neither do I, fully,' he said. 'My parents stopped telling me anything other than to stay away from the city or to stay in the house. And even as I go to the city and stand in the rain, and feel more alive, I come back and it's like I've been drained of everything.'

'Then why don't you leave? Why don't you just stay in the city?'

'When I spend too long away from the house I start to fade,' he said. 'Physically, I mean. That night when you found me standing in the rain, you were the only one that could see me,' he said. 'I'd tried to get on a bus, but the door closed on me. Tried to go inside a café, and I couldn't get in. Then you were there, and you could hear me, talk to me. That's when I realised, you must be like me.'

Maggie still didn't understand. Oscar was born, but he wasn't dead? He faded but he wasn't a ghost. And his mother, with the shroud, and her rasping voice, like one of the ghosts. And it all led back to Xavier. 'What did Xavier do?'

'I don't know,' Oscar said. 'But after I came home from the coffee shop, they wouldn't let me leave my room. One of them was always just there, watching. They said it was for my own good.' He was speaking very fast now, occasionally glancing at the door behind him. 'And then I really was sick. I've been sleeping endlessly, unable to get out of bed. But when my mother brought me breakfast this morning, she told me they had a very important visitor and just left. Usually, she stayed to make sure I ate, and then I'd go back to sleep all day. But she left in a hurry, to see you I guess, and I didn't eat the food. I wasn't really hungry. Then after a while, my mind just cleared. I felt awake again.'

'There was something in the tea they gave me, I think, to make me sleep. Maybe they gave you the same.'

Oscar grimaced. 'Yeah…maybe. I just don't understand why.'

'Why didn't you come down?'

'I didn't know what was going on, and I still felt weak,' he said. 'I listened at the door, then I heard a scream. By the time I got enough energy to peer through to the landing, they were carrying you up the stairs. I heard them lock you in.'

'How long has it been?'

'A few hours, at least. I pretended to be asleep when they came to check on me, then I've been waiting until it was clear to come and get you.'

'Why do they have me here?' she asked.

'I don't know,' he said again. How could he be as in the dark about this as she was?

'I have these memories, of being here. They didn't make sense before, but I think…I think Xavier killed my mother. I think he tried to do something to me, when I was younger.'

Oscar's face darkened and Maggie stepped towards him, put a hand on his arm. It was freezing cold, but she didn't let go. 'What aren't you telling me?'

'I think…' He sucked in a rattling breath. 'I think it might have to do with the noises in the basement.'

'What's in the basement?'

'I've never been allowed down there, and even though I've tried over the years, my mother always appears and stops me. Then I just wake up in my room again, hours lost from the day.'

'Oscar, that's awful.'

His face fell into shadow again, and he looked to the door behind him. 'I don't know why they brought you here, but it can't be for a good reason. We need to get you away from the house. And I know a way out. Do you trust me?'

Maggie squeezed his arm again and gave him a slight nod. 'Let's go.'

Oscar creaked the door open, and Maggie felt dizzy as she followed him out. He held a finger to his lips and paused on the landing, peering round to the grand staircase. She remained as quiet as she could, tiptoeing behind him and taking care with each step, testing the planks first before putting her whole weight on. There was a tapping somewhere in the house, the same as she'd heard downstairs. Where was it coming from? She looked out the window, the moonlight casting the night in a pale fog – no rain still. There was another oil lamp on one of the corner tables, so she grabbed it as quietly as she could, taking care not to drop this one. Oscar told her to stand for a moment while he checked downstairs. He moved as quiet as a ghost, and she noticed his shadow in the candlelight was fragmented, like there were two of them. There was another tap-tapping, and she peered her head round. Then she heard it – a wail that echoed from below. Oscar looked up at her, and then there was a hand on her shoulder. She spun round and her dad's ghost was there, staring down at her, his eyes darkened now into wide gaping holes. 'Run,' he rasped. 'She's coming.'

Maggie didn't wait for Oscar's signal. She ran down the stairs after him. Oscar stared back at her as she clattered down, his hands held up.

'What are you–'

'He said she's coming,' she said. 'We need to go.'

Oscar gave a single nod and ran to the front door. It was locked, and he began to undo the various mechanisms, but still it wouldn't open.

There was an echoing screech from down below, another wail, and then footsteps approaching. Maggie followed the sound to a cast iron door under the stairs, the basement. The sound of a key turning in the lock. She moved closer to Oscar and spoke quietly, desperately. 'A back door, window?'

He shook his head. 'All shuttered up.'

Maggie thought about what she'd seen of the house, the sitting room with the endless ceiling that didn't make sense, the room they'd had tea in. 'The window, overlooking the tree?'

'No, it's locked.'

She tugged him towards the drawing room anyway. 'Come on, let's go.'

'Maggie, we can't.'

'Glass can break,' she said, and he finally followed.

They ran together through to the sitting room, and Oscar closed the door behind, pulling a chair up against the door to hold it. She caught her reflection in the fractured mirror before the small side room, her hair ragged, skin white and goose-pimpled in the cold. Oscar looked worse, like he might disappear into his reflection at any moment. She carried on to the single window overlooking the ash tree and searched the space for something heavy. Her eyes landed on the bookcase. She picked up one of the books Xavier had been so precious about.

'Stand back,' she instructed Oscar who simply looked on as if frozen in time. She hurtled the tome as hard as she could against the glass, and it smashed through. Setting down the lamp, she wrapped her hand in the dressing gown and punched the rest of the pane through before climbing on the window seat and peering out. It wasn't a long drop, but it was straight into a thorny bramble bush. She was rethinking her options when there was a clatter from behind, and then a voice.

'Oscar, you stupid child, don't let her go,' the shrouded woman said, her words almost a hiss.

A hammering against the door.

'You don't know what you're doing,' his mother said to him. 'You'll die. If she leaves, it's all over. You won't survive any longer without her.'

Oscar glanced at Maggie and for a second she thought he was about to change his mind. That he would open the door and give her up, just like that. But he only moved to take off his jumper and put it over the broken pane. Then, he took some cushions from the seats and threw them into the brambles to soften their fall. With a nod to each other, Maggie leapt out into the undergrowth.

The thorns pierced through the fabric, scraping and piercing her skin. As she detangled herself, some of the thorns latched onto her, cutting and stinging into flesh. She pulled a couple of them out of her bare feet and rolled to the side. The ash tree groaned above her. Its branches moved inwards slightly as if it was trying to stop her from leaving. She tried standing up but stumbled backwards. She reached out with her bloodied hand to steady herself, grabbing onto the trunk of the tree. A sudden image filled her mind.

She can see herself, but as if from a distance, just a girl, many years before. She's crying, arm outstretched, blood dripping on a stone floor, and something else, a tree, though it's clad all in stone. It makes no sense. The room is dark, though, so it's hard to see, and there's a noise of something echoing, like the flutter of tiny wings, or the tapping of a thousand insect legs…moths, and she can feel them on her, crawling everywhere. Then, a voice chants, pulling her to look at the girl – her – again, as metal glints in the dark plunging downwards to her—

'Maggie!' Oscar's voice pulled her from the reverie. 'She's coming, I need to jump.'

Maggie blinked, confused, but moved away from the tree just as Oscar climbed onto the window ledge. His mother was just behind him now, her face still covered by the shroud.

'Now!' Maggie shouted.

He turned, looked once at her, then he rolled out of the window. He scrambled into the thorns with a few curses and heavy breaths. Maggie helped him out of the tangle of weeds as the woman stared down at them. Then she lifted her shroud, revealing a pale thin face It was so cracked at the edges that Maggie could see through her skin to exposed cheekbones, barely held together by thin threads of muscle and flesh. When she smiled, a large caterpillar crawled from her mouth and fell down into the brambles below. She pointed down at Oscar and let out a long rasping noise. Maggie didn't need to be warned twice, so she pulled Oscar up and they ran. As they hurtled down the pathway together, Oscar made a pained sound, and stopped. 'No, I can't come with you,' he said. 'I'll fade away in the city. I don't know if I can do it much longer.'

'I'll still be able to see you,' she said, her gaze darting back to the house. It would only be a matter of time before Oscar's parents followed. 'You can't stay here, not with them.'

He shook his head. 'I have to, I can't leave. I have no choice.'

'Of course you do,' she said, and pulled at his arm. 'We'll figure it out, we'll find a way.'

'I can hold them back for a bit, but you need to run, get out of here and never come back, okay?' he said. 'Maybe if you go far enough, you'll finally get away for good. You need to go as fast as you can, before the city and the forgetting takes hold. At least one of us should make it out of this cursed place.'

Maggie glanced back at Tair House, half obscured in the fog. Then there were bright lights at the front. Xavier's car lurching to life.

'We need to go, now,' she pleaded. 'Please.'

But he shook his head. 'You go, I'll try and stop him.'

As Oscar stood blocking the road by the first set of gates, Maggie finally gave in and sprinted down the gravelstone path. She glanced back to Oscar, watching as he was waving his arms at the car, at his father. Surely, he'd stop. Surely, he wouldn't run over his own son. But he wasn't slowing down. And Oscar didn't move. Maggie froze and watched on in horror as the car sped up.

'Oscar!' she cried out, and Oscar looked back at her slightly, his face grey, an expression contorted. 'He's not stop—'

Xavier drove straight into him. There was a sickening thud as Oscar rolled up and over the car, smashing the windscreen. A screech followed as Xavier's car swerved into the dry dead grass. Then, the engine whirred on, and he kept going.

Maggie screamed out and started running again. Trying

not to think of Oscar lying behind her, body bruised, battered and…no, this couldn't be happening. She was almost at the cemetery gates. She could see the rain there, a heavy torrent, loud and angry, as if hissing her forward. She ran faster, but the car's engine revved behind her. Xavier was going to reach her first. Just as the car sped into her path, Maggie leapt out of the way and landed awkwardly on her ankle. She cried out, rolling to the ground, feeling a painful pop. The car had stopped by the gates, the door opening, Xavier stepping out.

Another shadow settled beside her, a hand reaching out.

'Get up, Maggie. Run,' he said. Her father, still with her. Maggie peeled herself off the ground, ignoring the cuts and bruises, the thorns in her skin, the burning pain in her ankle, the ringing in her ears. Then with the car now blocking the gates she limped as fast as she could for the wall. She started climbing it, the stone rough on her skin as she scrambled to find a solid hold with her good foot. But her leg caught on a broken nail, cutting a clean line up her calf. A dizzying pain shot through her, and she bit down on her cheek to stop herself from passing out. She was almost at the top though. One more push, and she'd be over the wall. She could make it. She hauled herself up and swung a leg over the stone.

For a brief moment she felt the rain on her skin as she crossed the threshold of Tair House, felt the soothing chill of water run down one side of her, while the rest of her remained dry. Under a streetlamp in the distance, a ghost was watching, staring, a hand raised, pointing behind her. She was about to drop down to the other side when another hand grabbed her leg, grasping the cut with a sharp searing touch. Then it pulled her down into the dry dead earth below.

The House

When the girl, now a woman, stepped across the threshold of Tair House, finally back home, where she belonged, after all these years, the building took a long deep breath. The ash tree outside bent even further towards the walls, longing to be closer, to touch her, to feel her. Even the moths that had stayed dormant for too long, awoke.

The spirits within the house now stuck their heads out from the shadows, looked upon the girl that had started their life stuck in the house, in the forgotten inbetween. An endless purgatory that had crept into the city and infected it with the greyness and rain. The girl, now a woman, still bore the scar of the man of the house's first attempt at keeping her here forever. The spirits could see it in the way she rubbed her arm, and, in the way she looked into shadows, watched them move, able to see into the shadow world. For she too had spent time within it herself. Once, she had even been a part of this house, though she did not know any of that yet. The other residents in the house, the kind with their melted faces and put-together features, do not bear her any grievance, unlike the old man of the house. When they saw her step into the house, they waited and watched, wondering if they would have the strength to warn her when the time came.

Tair House has never been one to forget. Nor have those who live in the house — they are cursed to remember, in a place where time almost stands still, and where a dank dry dark is the order of every day. And the girl, now a woman, is starting to remember the memories she has learned to forget. They are a reminder of her intended fate, and of the darkness still to come.

Blood and ash

Maggie fell with a thud on the wrong side of the wall, the old man of the house with his hands on her legs, pulling, tugging. Maggie struggled and strained, but it was all in vain.

'You are a stubborn girl,' Xavier said. 'And now you've poisoned my son's mind. To think he'd rather die just so you might live your miserable existence in a city that will swallow you up anyway.'

'Get. Off. Me!'

She kicked at him, but Xavier was stronger than she'd imagined he could be. And then she realised. His hands were being guided by another. The shrouded woman, Oscar's mother was there too, holding her wrists in place. Maggie could smell the putrid rot of her body. Her hands like ice, sharp fingers burning into her skin. Then it was like something was crawling on her skin, the scurry of a hundred tiny feet. Caterpillars, dropping from her mouth and onto her body, moving towards her wounds. Maggie retched. It was suddenly difficult to breathe, the air cold and sharp in her throat.

'You will learn your place, Maggie, my dear, your purpose,' he said. 'Do you remember, now? What your mother did? How she ruined everything.'

'Let me go,' she wailed.

'Your grandmother kept the inevitable from happening for too long, it's time to put things right.'

'Did you kill her?' Maggie spat back. 'My mother?'

Xavier didn't answer as he took thick rope and bound her wrists, then he and Lucia dragged her up the driveway even as she resisted. At the first gate, she saw Oscar's body slumped on the ground. Blood pooled in the corner of his lips and his leg was bent at an awkward angle. His eyes were wide open, staring at her. Unmoving. 'You killed him,' she said.

'No. He'll be fine. No thanks to you.'

'He's dead.'

'He was already halfway there,' Xavier said. 'But soon he won't be again, if you do as you're told for once.'

'Why are you doing this?'

'Hush, child.' It wasn't Xavier that spoke this time, but the shrouded woman. Her voice was a rasp like the Green Man on the street. 'Hush.'

Maggie screamed again, and then the shrouded woman had her hands on her mouth and nose, squeezing hard. 'Hush. Hush, child. Don't cry. This will all be over soon.'

Maggie was unable to breathe. White dots swirled in her eyes and the last thing she saw before she passed out was the face of the shrouded woman smiling, ash and moths spilling from the cracks in her face.

*

It was cold and quiet when Maggie awoke with a strangled breath. She gasped out as if she'd only just now remembered to breathe, the memory of the shrouded woman's hands on her face. Her wrists were still bound, tied now to a chain on the wall. Up and to her left was a crack of light coming from a staircase, but other than that everything was pitch black. She was in the basement.

There was a thick cloying rotting scent in the air. It was something she'd only experienced once before. The day she'd come to visit her gran only to find her sitting in her chair, no longer breathing. The undertaker had said she'd died peacefully, probably in her sleep, but maybe they just said that to families, because why say anything different to cause more pain. She wondered now if during her gran's last moment whether she regretted anything that had happened. Whether she wished she would have told Maggie about her past and about this house. Maybe if she had, Maggie wouldn't have answered Xavier's call. If she'd not come here, maybe she wouldn't be about to die, in the dark, surrounded by death, ghosts, and rotting things.

She screamed out, called for help. No answer. 'Xavier! Oscar!' Then, 'Dad?'

No answer. Even the ghosts had abandoned her. She fussed at her wrists, tried to bite into the rope with her teeth, but she only ended up with sharp threads on her tongue. She spat them out and curled up into herself, pulling her knees to her chest. It was only after a few moments of sitting in silence that she heard it. A breath, somewhere in the room with her. Was it the shrouded woman?

She leaned forward slightly, crawled as far as she could get before the chains were too taut to move further. She held her breath and listened, and there it was again. A breath. Slow, hoarse, but there was definitely someone – *something* – here with her.

'Hello?' she whispered, struggling to speak. 'Who's there?'

Maggie thought about what Xavier had said about Oscar. That he wasn't really dead. Had they locked him in here with her too? 'Oscar, is that you? It's me, Maggie. Are you…can you hear me?'

There was a pause punctuated only by a small echoey sound of footsteps that came from above. A drop of water fell on her cheek, and when she looked up dew-drops glittered slightly where the small shaft of light from under the door shone. Then, in the corner she spotted a flurry of tiny eyes. More moths, bigger than any she'd seen in her life, gathered across the dimly lit wall. Maggie tugged on the chain again, and as it rattled a flurry of something flew at her face. She tried to bat it away. The moth circled her then finally landed on her leg. Then another followed, settling on her sweat and blood-marked skin. They fluttered from above and below. Was that what she'd heard, not a breath but moth wings? She thought about the creatures that had fallen from Lucia's cheeks and shuddered.

She'd read once that moths were messengers of death. That they lived in dark indeterminate spaces because that's where they were from, a place where a blackness was absolute. Maybe they were a harbinger of what was to come for her.

Maggie sat curled up as tears fell silently down her cheeks, and a moth landed on her hand, crawled up to one of the thorn-cuts. She could just see the dim outline of it, wings outstretched on her hand, furry legs patting up and down as if trying to comfort her. Its head bowed towards the blood, and…was it drinking it? She shot her hand out to push it away. It took flight, so close to her ears she could almost hear it whisper, before flying back to settle on the wall behind. She had a distinct feeling it was watching her.

Then, came a humming noise. A voice, disjointed. Wordless, but Maggie remembered the words. She'd heard the song before, in her childhood, played on the piano.

'Rain Rain go away,' she whispered through her tears. 'But it's always raining.'

The humming stopped then the voice came again. 'Maggie, little Maggie wants to play. My darling sunshine. Even rain must have an end.'

Maggie could hardly breathe. Her heart hammering against her chest. 'M-Mum?'

'I told you never to come back, my sunshine. Don't come back,' she said. 'Don't come back,' and her voice trailed off into another humming song.

'Are you…' Maggie took a deep breath. 'Are you a ghost?'

There was a deep inhale of breath. 'I don't know. I don't remember. The house takes so much from me. If I was dead, wouldn't it be more peaceful? Would I still be able to feel pain? So much pain, Maggie. Can you make it stop? Can you make it go away?'

'Have you been down here, all this time?' Maggie was horrified by the thought of it. She'd hardly been here minutes, and she'd give anything to be gone from this dark chasm. Where moths whispered, and the stone floors held such a sharp coldness that it felt like it was seeping into skin and bones.

'Why did you come back here, Maggie?'

'Xavier, he tricked me. I wanted to find out why…why I can see ghosts, why you were gone.'

Her mum paused for a few moments. 'You sound older, sweetheart,' she said.

'I'm almost thirty.'

'Oh. Has it been that long? Time is strange in this place. Sometimes I'm awake, trapped down here, and sometimes I'm somewhere else.'

The thought of it all made Maggie want to reach out into the dark, to hold her Mum again, to tell her it was going to be okay. Was this to be her fate too? Held in the dark by a mad man and a woman that was half-ghost.

'He always said he would find you eventually,' she said.

'His son found me first,' Maggie said. 'He didn't know who I was, but we had things in common. It's not his fault though, he's…' She tried to shake away the image that popped into her head, of Oscar lying on the ground, blood pooling around his mouth, eyes grey with a blank stare. She couldn't bear the idea of him dead – and that somehow, it was her fault.

'Did you ever leave the city?'

'No,' Maggie replied. 'I don't think I could.'

'Hmm. Yes. It's this house, the curse,' she said, a finality in her voice. 'It's trapped us all.'

'In this city where it rains,' Maggie said distantly.

There was a long silence during which Maggie only listened to the slow hiss of her mother's breath. Part of her wanted there to be more light so she could see her properly again, though she was scared of what she might see. How much had her mother changed in over two decades of being trapped in such a place? 'Why has he done this?'

'I suppose he blames me. For what happened to Lucia.'

'The shrouded woman?'

'Yes,' she said. 'She and Xavier came to the house when I was just a girl, you know, to put on a show.' There was a pause, as her mum seemed to try and catch her breath.

'She was his assistant?' Maggie said, piecing it together. The Fearless Ferrante, Lucia, his fearless love.

'It was all my fault,' her mum continued. 'I was scared, and I interrupted the performance. Then it all happened so fast, and there was a fire. She died, and something weakened here, between the living and dead in Tair House.' She paused again, then said the next part slowly, as if the words were pulled from a dream. 'It's funny, I can see it so clearly, like I was watching myself from afar. I didn't remember it at all when I met Xavier, when he invited me to his party, told me about his gift. But I've had so much time to think down here. So much time to remember, and this house, it holds all things close. Memories, pain. It talks to me, helps me see things clearly, helps me see through the clouds and the rain. I suppose I'm a part of the house now too. I need it, as much as it needs me.'

'I don't understand,' Maggie said.

'Don't worry sweetheart, in time the pain lessens,' she said. 'It's just like going to sleep. And sometimes, in your dreams you'll remember the good times. So clearly, as if you're watching someone else's life.'

'But I don't want to be part of this,' Maggie said. 'I want to go home.'

'You are home, sweetheart,' she said, and started to hum the nursery rhyme again, in a soft voice, slightly out of tune.

Maggie closed her eyes and listened, and imagined she was anywhere but in the basement, with a mother that may or not be a ghost, trying not to think about what lay beyond her in the dark.

*

Maggie wasn't sure how long she'd been sitting there with her mum, humming or singing, or just breathing, when a key jangled in the heavy door above. The door creaked open, and Maggie shielded her eyes as the light streamed in. The figure that stood there was dressed in a black hooded cloak. He held an oil lamp in one hand, and a large book in the other. Maggie noticed that the leather of it was damaged – the one she'd thrown from the window. Behind him, came Lucia, the Fearless Ferrante, the shrouded woman, and they climbed down the stairwell together, as if in a wedding procession. As the lamp illuminated the cavernous space around her, Maggie screamed.

Finally, she could see her mum clearly. She was all skin and bones, wrapped in the roots of the ash tree that had broken through the foundations of the basement, its dark tendrils twisting and breaking the stone apart. In some places she couldn't tell where the tree's roots ended and her mum's limbs begun. Her skin was mottled with lichen, and her hair was long and knotted, as black as the soil. But, she wasn't a ghost. She looked alive. Her arm was the only exposed part of her that looked like skin. It had been pinned to the side and attached to the wall with a chain. On the forearm, two triangles had been carved intersecting slightly at the bottom, dark blood dripping gradually onto the roots of the tree below her.

'Mum,' Maggie whispered.

Her mum's eyes cracked open, and she craned her neck just a little to take Maggie in. It was hard to tell if she was smiling or grimacing as she did.

'You're a monster!' Maggie screamed now at Xavier. 'What have you done to her?'

'Hush, child,' the shrouded woman said.

'Yes, Maggie, my dear,' Xavier said. 'Please, calm down.'

'Calm down?' Maggie flailed and tugged at her own chain

again. 'Don't tell me to calm down, and I'm sure as *hells* not your dear!' The echo of the chain rattling disturbed some of the moths above and they flurried downwards in flight, bodies flashing crimson in the darkness, before settling on her mum's body, camouflaging with the lichen. A caterpillar emerged from between the roots, moved across her mum's brow, before burying beneath her eyelid. Another crawled into her ear, but her mum barely flinched. Maggie felt like her world was spinning. She was dizzy, sick.

Xavier let out a non-committal chuckle as if the entire horrific scene was amusing. 'Stop struggling and fussing, you'll need your energy,' he said, coming closer to her. The oil lamp cast strange shadows across the walls, and the light illuminated a range of marks, some looking as if they'd been purposefully carved into the stone: triangles in different variations, almost like the scar on Maggie's arms.

'Lucia, my love, is the house ready?'

Lucia, the shrouded woman, the Fearless Ferrante, nodded. Then she drifted to the tree and knelt by her mum's side. She touched her cheek and smiled. 'Hush, child, hush, little Evelyn, you've done so well,' Lucia said.

'I'm so tired, Lucia,' her mum said. 'Will it be over soon?'

'Yes, soon. Very soon.'

'The house is so hungry,' her mum continued. 'I can feel what it wants, and I don't have enough to give it anymore. I'm too weak.'

'Not to worry,' Xavier said. 'We only need more of your flesh and blood.'

Lucia turned to Maggie with her crooked smiled, and as Maggie struggled, Xavier loosened her from her chains and dragged her across the floor to beside the ash tree. Lucia took her arm and held it to the tree, then she traced her fingers to the place where Maggie's broken triangle scar was. As she touched the uneven skin, a burning pain spread up Maggie's arm and she screamed out.

'Ah, yes,' Lucia said, unfazed. 'That which first gave me strength.' She inhaled and her face flickered, her features rearranging into something more solid, less broken. Then Maggie noticed the creatures crawling between the cracks, weaving silk-like strands, knitting threads together across her jaw, forming a soft sheer skin.

Xavier stood before them and opened his book. Inside, Maggie could see the mark of the two triangles, upside down, intersecting at the edges.

Her scar, unfinished.

'I call upon the spirit realm, the otherworld, the land between, to answer our call,' Xavier began.

'Stop!' Maggie cried out, but Lucia put her arm over her mouth again. The rancid taste of her cold skin stuck in her mouth, making her gag, but she couldn't move. She was forced to watch on as Xavier continued. Next to her, her mother was singing in a rasping voice, '*rain rain, go away,*' again.

'Hear us, spirit realms. We come to you to offer a sacrifice, a conduit so that we may continue to live in this house, so that the door may remain ever open,' Xavier said.

'*Come again another day,*' her mum was singing.

Xavier turned and whispered to Lucia, 'So that my dearest love and my family, may stay here with me forever more. Give us that power to be together again.' Maggie heard the crack of Lucia's jaw and another caterpillar dropped from her mouth, landing on Maggie's lap. Maggie grimaced, kicking and wriggling, but Lucia's hold was firm.

'*Little Maggie wants to play.*' Her mum's voice grew stronger, but Xavier and Lucia were paying her no mind. Maggie tried to twist her neck to look, but she was held down still. She felt like her jaw might break under Lucia's grip.

Xavier put the heavy book on the ground next to the oil lamp and took out a sharp knife from a sheath at his side. He held it out with both hands, the glint of it reflecting the lamplight. 'Let blood turn to ash, and ash to blood, to bring my family back to me. Let the rift awake again, and the dead walk free amongst the living. Let the house stand strong, while the city rains.' Lucia let go, so she could take Xavier's hand, both of them looming down on her now.

'*Rain rain go away, come again another day.*'

Maggie looked between her mum whose eyes were closed, with an uneven smile on her face, then up to Xavier.

'Please,' she said. 'Please, don't.'

Xavier knelt down at her side knife in hand, a focussed look in his eyes. He cut the ropes first, then as Lucia took one arm, he took the other and pinned it to the tree. He was whispering some words under his breath, an enchantment or ritual, Maggie was unsure. One of the tree roots moved beneath her, twisted up and wrapped itself around her wrist, binding her in place. Xavier traced the line of the triangle with his finger, first.

'Let the symbol be full,' he said. 'Your connection to the spirit realm will be complete.' With a precise movement, he cut into Maggie's arm. The pain was intense, and she cried out.

Roots tightened around her arm. The tree was pulling Maggie into an embrace, just like it had her mother. As the lamplight shone on Lucia's form, Maggie watched as the shrouded woman's grey skin began to glow with colour. As she took the shroud from her face, her hair too, started to shine. She was even smiling wide, redness returning to her lips and cheeks. As Maggie bled, Lucia was awakened, and Maggie could feel the house around her breathe, feel the stone vibrate with the sting of her wound.

It pulled her closer, further in beside her mother who took her other hand in hers, fingers thin and rough like they were the ragged roots themselves. At least she wasn't alone.

Maggie peered around Xavier and saw now the myriad figures standing behind him. More ghosts, their faces distorted as if they were standing in the rain. There were two older ones that shared features with her mum – her grandparents perhaps, then her dad standing beside them. Gradually, they became more solid, like she could finally see them clearly as she bled. Was her blood keeping the door to the spirit realm open? Or was she a part of the realm now herself?

Her dad moved closer to them and put his hand to her mum's cheek, and she smiled at his touch.

Then her dad leaned and whispered to her. 'Maggie. It's not too late. You must free us.'

'I don't know how.'

'I remember the fire,' Maggie's mum said, her eyes closed. 'On the night Lucia died. They never should have put it out.'

And as Maggie twisted her neck to look at her mum, the image of it was suddenly clear in her mind too.

The ritual, her grandparents, the gathered guests running away, and her mother, just a child crying in the corner. Xavier, a young man, standing over Lucia, lying on the ground with dazzling beauty, a belly slightly raised. Pregnant. She's surrounded by smoke and ash now, as the house around them burns. Xavier lifts her to safety, pulls her outside where people are crying, screaming. Sirens trill in the distance. To the crowd, she looks like she's sleeping, but Maggie can see her clearly now. She can't wake up. She is stuck, in the in-between. On the other side, screaming a never-ending scream.

Maggie understood now too, knew what it was to see into the abyss of the in-between. She'd been there before. Back when she lived in this house, after her dad died, and Xavier had moved into it.

Her mind spun again in a smoky haze, and she could see herself this time, as a young girl, watching as if it had been recorded on film. Xavier was dragging her down, kicking and screaming into the basement...

She cries as he chains her to the tree, just like she is chained now, and she doesn't understand, because she is so little, so young, she can't even struggle. He begins the cut on her arm, chants the words. Then something else is in the room with her. A darkness, and in it, a woman standing, wearing a shroud. She had been trapped, but now she's free. And then, a room full of ghosts, spilling out around her. She screams out. Wants it all to be over. Wants to be with her mum, wants her dad to go away, because he's in the room with her and that doesn't make any sense, because he's dead already, and she can't be seeing him, not here, not with that face with sunken eyes and thin cheeks. She screams again and there are footsteps from above. Someone is coming down for her. Her mum, with heavy footsteps, running. Before Xavier can move, she launches herself at Xavier, hits him with something heavy – a cuckoo clock across the head, and it breaks in a final 'cu-ckoo, cu-ckoo', and the bird hangs limp, clock hands stuck as it strikes midnight. But it worked, his grip is broken. Her mum tugs her free from the tree, scoops her up into her arms and runs. Whispers, 'We don't have long, she's coming. But don't worry sweetheart, I'm going to get you out of here. I love you, you'll never know how much.'

She runs and runs, to where she meets her Gran, standing in the rain. Her mum passes her over, tells them not to come back.

Maggie has seen this all before, a sense of déjà vu creeping in. She watches herself carried away, and she wants to tell her mum to go with her, to leave Tair House, to not go back. But her mum is resolute in her returning. She stands and turns back to the house, runs to it. Maggie is seeing now, no longer only remembering.

Maggie follows the gaze of the house, as if she were there the entire time, as if she wasn't being carried away into the city, like this is happening now, and will happen again. Her mum is muttering something under her breath. There's something in her pocket. Matches, and a bottle of alcohol. She's looking at the ash tree and she pours the alcohol over the roots.

'Only flames can swallow ash,' she says. And she lights the match. But it never reaches the roots. The shrouded woman is upon her before it catches alight, and her mum will wake up back here, underneath the tree, forever to be bound to the house as the ghosts and greyness and rain seep out.

And then the image so stark, of her mum bound to the roots, bleeding, as a scream echoes from above. Maggie can see it all so clearly. As if she is the house, and the house is her, and her mum and Lucia are a part of it too.

Her vision stretches once more into the drawing room above, the room where it all began, and Xavier is cradling Lucia in his arms. 'Push, Lucia my love,' and Maggie finds herself willing it too, the house wants this as much as Lucia does, push, push, just a little further. And she does. Blood and cries, as a baby is born, a boy, gazing up at the world with his grey-silver eyes, changing colours depending on the light of the room.

'It's impossible,' the man of the house says. 'Our miracle, our boy.'

And the couple embrace, hold hands, cradle their son that had been reborn from death. Though, even in his first breaths, the boy's eyes are looking behind him, to the family of ghosts that watch on, with tears in their eyes. One family traded for another. And the house will do what it can to protect him, to keep him safe.

Maggie let out a long gasp as she woke again, eyes blinking rapidly. No one has moved, and only a few seconds must have passed, though it felt like hours.

Time is different here, her mum had said. *Time moves slow.*

Maggie tensed her hands to the roots, realising she is now a part of the house, a part of its memories. But she wouldn't be a part of the ones it had yet to make. She remembered her mum's words as her gaze moving around the room, and she whispered, 'Only flames can swallow ash.'

Only flames

The basement seemed to shrink as in front of her Xavier and Lucia were embracing. Lucia was starting to look more and more like her old self, the Fearless Ferrante, Xavier's medium's assistant, awake again, to live by Maggie's sacrifice. She'd died here, and never left. Now that Maggie had seen it all, she felt a tug of pity. She felt part of the loss as if it were her own, though she knew it was just the house in her head, messing with her memories. The house that had bound itself to her, her mum, and ultimately, Lucia. Time, it said, was supposed to heal wounds, but here, in this house, it had allowed them to fester. Allowed the rot of it to ooze into everything, until all that was left was pain and bitterness. Maggie could feel it even now, doubt creeping into her thoughts, wrestling with her to just let go. Would it be so bad, she found herself thinking, to just close her eyes and go to sleep. She'd be with her mum, her dad not far away either.

No, that was the house talking. She didn't want to die. And she didn't want to be trapped here, bound to the same fate her mother had. Then after she'd been used up, would they find someone else? She didn't want Xavier to win. She scoured the room, eyes settling on the oil lamp on the ground, next to

Xavier's precious book. There was a scent too, of the dressing gown she'd borrowed from her mother's room, soaked in the oil from the spilled lamp in her room.

Only flames…

She reached out her feet slowly, tried to hook the lamp with her toes. She was mere inches away. If she could slip down just a little.

But Lucia was watching her with a smile, watching her struggle like a fly caught in a spider's web. She probably thought Maggie was just trying to escape, to break free.

Above her, there was a creak of footsteps as if someone was moving around upstairs, and her heart leapt. Her focus returned to the room. For a mad moment, she wondered if Angus had found her. If he'd called the police and was about to walk in, Arlo in his arms, sniffing out her scent to bring her home. But when the door opened, another shadowy figure stood at the top. Oscar. He was whole again, his limbs no longer misshapen, only the blood on his clothes evidence of what his father had done.

'Son,' Xavier said, calling up. 'Come, join us.'

With his parents' attention on him, Maggie had the time she needed. She stretched out, feeling pain in her shoulder as a tightening root dug into her skin. She bit down on her lip to fight the pain, tasting blood in her mouth. But she carried on. She was almost there.

Oscar was coming down the stairs and his parents were readying to welcome him with open arms. Their son, reborn again, to live in this house for a time, together. Maggie pushed the thoughts of the house away, as they tried to welcome him too, and focused her mind on the task. She slid down and caught the side of the lamp with her bare feet and pulled.

The heat of it burned her toes, but she didn't let go. She just gripped tighter and pulled. Then, when it was close enough, next to the tie of her dressing gown, she hooked her stronger ankle around the side of it. As Xavier and Lucia turned their gaze towards her once more, she smiled. They tried to stop her, but they were too late. She kicked the lamp into herself. It smashed, and the flame caught.

The room ignited in a whirr of heat and pain. It licked across her skin, but she felt the roots around her slacken, and there was a screech from somewhere. Maggie scrambled, slipping out of the dressing gown, and away from the fire. The flames were spreading fast and far now, into the ash tree.

She tried to free her mother from it, but her father only appeared beside her and shook his head. 'It's our time, sunshine,' he said. 'Leave this place, live a happy life. We ove you.' And before she could reply, he leaned into the flames, embracing her mother. They were subsumed together by the burning tree.

The stones around her were cracking too, and a flurry of moths flew into the air and began retreating to the door at the top of the stairs. Caterpillars scurried across the ceiling, searching for cracks within the wall to escape the heat.

And Xavier looked the most panicked and crazed of them all. He was batting at the air while Lucia's form was crumbling. She was looking at her hands and her face was melting as if she was one of Maggie's ghosts in the rain.

'Xavier,' she said. 'It's not my time.' And then she sunk into herself, every part of her gone, turning to ash beneath her husband's feet. In the middle of the basement stair, Oscar had frozen, his figure a silhouette. He was shielding his face from the smoke, eyes moving between Xavier and the remains of his mother.

The flames were too hot now, and Xavier looked at Maggie with wild eyes, stood between her and Oscar. Stood between her and her escape.

'Just let me go home, please, this can all be over,' she shouted.

'No, this isn't over until she's back with me,' he said, half an eye on the ashes beneath his feet. 'She has to come back!'

He took the knife from his sheathe again, but Maggie had her own play – she picked up the ritual book and held it over the burning ash tree. 'I'll burn this,' she said. 'If you don't let me leave.'

Xavier flinched and considered her for just a few seconds, then he lunged at her. She dropped the book, and it caught aflame. Xavier let out an exasperated gasp and tried to pull it from the flames.

'We'll find another way,' he said, aiming the knife at her. 'If I spill all your blood at once, maybe she'll come back.' He started towards her.

'It's over,' she said, sidling towards the stairs, trying to put as much distance as she could between them. 'It's done. Just let this go.'

'You killed her,' he said. 'You ignorant girl, you spoiled little brat. It's all your fault, and your stupid bitch of a mother.'

'This was you! It was always you, and this house, and your tricks. I didn't ask for this, my mother didn't ask for this.' Maggie held her hand to her mouth, the smoke now burning her throat and eyes. She had to go, now. But if she turned her back on him, he'd surely catch her.

'Your family are cursed,' he said. 'And you all deserve to burn.'

He made to lurch for her, but something stopped him. His

leg was caught, and he tripped. A root, or a hand reaching out from the burning remains of the ash tree, it was hard to tell. And then the stone was cracking, falling in. Maggie didn't need another sign to leave, and as Xavier disappeared under a flurry of smoke and stone, she sprinted to the stairs and ran up before the whole basement caved in. The steps groaned, and the wood splintered. As she reached Oscar, he grabbed her hand, and together they ascended to the landing. Maggie shut the door behind.

'My parents,' Oscar said, distantly as they stood there, out of breath, coughing from the fumes.

'Oscar…I'm sorry.'

Oscar stared at the door, the key in hand and locked it. Then, together, with Oscar helping her to stay upright, they ran from the damned house, as the walls began to crack and crumble, falling into itself like a sinkhole was pulling everything down into the earth. Outside it, the ash tree flared, sending smoke rising into the air. Then, as the smoke broke through the clouds the rain began. Drop after drop until it was a downpour, extinguishing the fire and leaving behind only broken stone, charred wood, and smoke. At the gate to the cemetery, Oscar stopped. He took her hand and looked her up and down. 'You look awful.'

She couldn't help but smile. 'Thanks. So do you.' His hair was slightly singed at the edges, his pale cheeks smudged with ash and rain. She reached to wipe away a mark beneath his eye, and found his skin was as cold as the air in Tair House. She could hardly believe that just hours ago she'd seen him lying dead by this very spot, blood pooling at the corner of his mouth. Yet here was, standing in front of her, whole again, lips slightly quirked in a pained smile.

'You're bleeding, too,' he added, and he took out a pocket square from his coat and started to wrap it around her arm.

'Guess I'll have another scar,' she said, wincing slightly as he tied the edges in a knot. Her other arm was burnt badly too, and it stung with the hiss of the rain, though the cold was also soothing. She was bloodied and bruised, but she'd made it out of Tair House alive. Just. 'Thank you. For helping me. In there, too.'

Oscar's head dipped slightly. 'I'm sorry about…about everything. About what they did, about your parents,' he said. 'I don't understand it.'

Maggie took a deep breath. 'I think he was trying to keep you and your mother alive, after she died.'

'But I'm here,' he said. 'And she's gone, dead. Again. So what does that mean for me?'

'You were born here, right, maybe that's the difference,' she said, hoping with everything she had left that she was right. 'You're not like her.'

'My father said I was dying, that I needed the house,' he said, staring back at his broken old home. He'd been a captive there almost as much as her mother had. How would he move on after this?

Maggie placed a hand on his arm and pulled him back to look at her. 'You look pretty good to me.' But then, in the rain something changed. As the water trickled down his skin, and he wiped his brow on his sleeve, Oscar's face appeared grey, distorted.

'Oscar…' she leaned in to touch his face, but he moved to look over her shoulder.

'Do you see it?' he said. 'It's so beautiful. The sunrise.'

Maggie turned to look towards the city where a red sky

blared above its jagged silhouette. It was the first time she'd seen the whole sky in years, the clouds making way for a long horizon. It was beautiful. 'Hey, maybe we can leave the city together, now,' she said, a tear falling down her cheek. 'Or swim across the sea, just like you wanted.' But Maggie knew even before she turned back and saw only light footprints on the ground beside her, marks already disappearing with the rain, that Oscar too, was gone.

After the rain

The city had a different type of thrum. The kind that buzzed
with chatter and traffic, tourists and visitors thronging the
streets. Summer had finally arrived, and the sun shone rays of
gold on the old stone buildings in the centre, clearing away the
grey tendrils that had for so long crept out from Tair House,
infected the city with the rain.

Maggie walked down the cobbled streets, past her usual
ghostly waypoints and felt a mix of loss and relief as no ghosts
appeared in front of her. Things were back to how they should
be, how they should always have been. She hoped the ghosts,
like Oscar and her parents, had gone to a better place, to meet
the sunrise.

Her memories of the house were still clear in her mind
– she wasn't sure she'd ever forget the image of her parents
swallowed by flames, of the shrouded woman with her moth-
holed face, or of Xavier, the man who'd brought the curse
upon them. But somehow, the sunshine went some way to
making things right. Set a clarity in her mind, allowing her to
move on.

She headed towards The Undercroft, enjoying the touch of
warmth on her skin, the trill of summer birdsong. A busker

was playing a guitar on the street outside the bar, and she stopped for a while, watched him, his case full of coins.

She descended finally to the basement room and entered with a smile and a wave. Angus was tending the bar, and she noticed the absence of shadow by his brother's favourite stool. It was quiet, which was perhaps unsurprising for such a sunny day. It would fill up at night, maybe even more so if people began to yearn for the dark in the absence of it.

'Hey Angus, told you I'd come back.'

Angus put down the glass he was polishing and approached her, looked her up and down with a frown, then he scratched the back of his neck. 'You from that distillery up north? Been ages since we've had a delivery, was about to file a complaint.'

'Angus?' Maggie said. 'It's me.'

'Aye, I see, well, where's the delivery then?'

Maggie stood silent at first, unsure what to say. But it was clear he'd forgotten her. Maybe it was to do with the rain, and the house. Without it, the city's slate was wiped clean. The purgatory that had taken hold had ended, and it was time for the living to start again.

She put her hand out. 'Nice to meet you,' she said. 'I'm Maggie. I'm not from the distillery, I was actually here about the job?'

'Job?'

'Yeah, I'm a great bartender, whisky connoisseur, even.'

He didn't look convinced. 'Where'd you work last?'

'Similar place to this, cocktails, whisky specials, that sort of thing,' she said.

'Hmm,' he said. 'As it happens, I have been looking for someone new. All my staff seemed to have just disappeared over night. Must be the economy.'

'Well, I'm here, and I think we'd get on great.'

'You're a confident lass,' he said. 'But I appreciate that and forthrightness. Why don't we do a trial shift and see how we go?'

'Excellent, shall we start now?'

Angus's eyebrows almost merged together as he gave the empty bar a cursory look. 'How about you start by making me an old fashioned. That shouldn't be too hard with your experience.'

Maggie smiled and nodded, and she headed over to the bar, quickly gathered what she needed, and made the perfect drink. Angus watched her with a bemused expression, his hand occasionally jolting as if he wanted to step in and show her where something was, but she was a step ahead of him every time. When she served up the drink, Angus took a small sip. He paused for a moment in a slow nod, then he looked up at her with an 'oh go on then' expression, then he said, 'You're hired. We can do a run through of the brands later, what goes well with what. Oh, and don't use that Jack Daniels,' he said. 'I just keep it there for-'

'Tourists with no taste?' Maggie completed.

'Aye, exactly,' he said with a familiar smile.

Maggie found her gaze lingering on the bottle, though, thinking of Oscar. After work, she'd go to visit him and her family at the cemetery and tell them about her day. It was a new routine she found comfort in, a way to remember her ghosts, to make sure she'd never forget them like she once had. But these were different kind of ghosts for her now. They were the kind she couldn't see but could still hold close in her memories, as she traversed this city, where it sometimes, but not always, rained.

*

At the weekend, Maggie bought a train ticket to the first destination that caught her eye on the station board and took a trip out of the city. The journey along the coast was marked by clear blue skies, the curve of land meeting the sea, and not a single cloud upon the horizon. At a quiet beach in a small coastal village, Maggie stood looking across the water as she wrapped Oscar's pocket square around her wrist. Then, she stepped into the sea. Around her, the cool water embraced her. And when she put her head beneath the water to swim for the first time in years, the only thing she saw was the sediment and sand glittering in the afternoon sun.

Discover Luna Novella in our store:

https://www.lunapresspublishing.com/shop

www.ingramcontent.com/pod-product-compliance
Lightning Source LLC
Chambersburg PA
CBHW032016180726
48283CB00008B/2706